RAINS OF REMORSE

LANTERN BEACH ROMANTIC SUSPENSE, BOOK 5

CHRISTY BARRITT

River Heights

COMPLETE BOOK LIST

Squeaky Clean Mysteries:

Lantern Beach Romantic Suspense

Tides of Deception

Shadow of Intrigue

Storm of Doubt

Winds of Danger

Lantern Beach P.D.

On the Lookout

Attempt to Locate

First Degree Murder

Dead on Arrival

Plan of Action

Lantern Beach Escape

Afterglow (a novelette)

Lantern Beach Blackout

Dark Water

Carolina Moon Series

Home Before Dark

Gone By Dark

Wait Until Dark

Light the Dark

Taken By Dark

Suburban Sleuth Mysteries:
Death of the Couch Potato's Wife

Fog Lake Suspense:
Edge of Peril
Margin of Error
Brink of Danger
Line of Duty (coming soon)

Cape Thomas Series:
Dubiosity
Disillusioned
Distorted

Standalone Romantic Mystery:
The Good Girl

Suspense:
Imperfect
The Wrecking

Sweet Christmas Novella:
Home to Chestnut Grove

Standalone Romantic-Suspense:
Keeping Guard

The Last Target

Race Against Time

Ricochet

Key Witness

Lifeline

High-Stakes Holiday Reunion

Desperate Measures

Hidden Agenda

Mountain Hideaway

Dark Harbor

Shadow of Suspicion

The Baby Assignment

The Cradle Conspiracy

Trained to Defend

Nonfiction:

Characters in the Kitchen

Changed: True Stories of Finding God through Christian Music (out of print)

The Novel in Me: The Beginner's Guide to Writing and Publishing a Novel (out of print)

CHAPTER ONE

REBECCA JARVIS STEPPED into her house, deposited her purse on the table by the door, and paused.

As remnants of the rain shower cooled her exposed skin, the hair on her neck rose.

Something felt different, felt off. But what?

She scanned her surroundings. Everything looked just as she'd left it.

The Christmas tree glimmered in the corner, handmade ornaments decorating each branch. Diapers and wipes from a recent baby shower formed a small cityscape on the dining room table. The savory scent of Boatman's Stew wafted from the kitchen, where she had left it in a Crockpot before going to work.

Nothing seemed out of place.

But Rebecca would be a fool to dismiss the feeling in her gut. Her subconscious whispered secrets she couldn't quite hear.

Had someone else been in her house?

She sucked in a quick breath at the thought. That couldn't be the case. A mix of pregnancy hormones and an overactive imagination left her feeling paranoid.

She took a step back and rubbed her belly, murmuring words of comfort to the baby nestled in her womb. "It's going to be okay. Mama's not going to let anything happen to you, Sweet Pea."

Should she call the police?

As her head wobbled, Rebecca leaned on the entryway table and briefly closed her eyes. She couldn't call the police just because of a gut feeling. Most likely, this was nothing. For some reason, she'd felt so overwhelmed lately, and she could hardly think straight.

That settled it. She was being ridiculous. Nothing was wrong here.

She was about to become a single mom, and that meant she needed to get used to being the man and the woman of the family. There would be no one here to protect her and Emma—all of that fell on Rebecca's shoulders.

She swallowed hard at the thought, trying to ignore the despair that nipped at her.

Cautiously, Rebecca took a step forward. The floor creaked beneath her weight.

She paused again. Listened.

There was nothing. No sounds. Nothing out of place.

If only she could lose that nagging feeling in her gut.

She took another step, staying close to the wall. Slipping into the kitchen, she reached into the wooden bucket she kept on the floor and grabbed a rolling pin. She gripped it like a bat and drew in a shaky breath.

Call the police.

The thought whispered through her mind again. But she couldn't.

She didn't have a reasonable excuse as to why the cops should come. Her front door had been locked, nothing appeared to be out of place, and there were no signs anyone had been inside.

Most likely, this was nothing. Maybe a critter of some sort had gotten inside through the attic or the heat had come on, the air coming through the vents causing a false sense of movement.

That was probably it.

But Rebecca needed to be sure.

She swallowed hard, hoping that in ten minutes she would feel ridiculous. That she would prop her feet up, close her eyes for a few seconds, and listen to some Christmas music—all things she'd been daydreaming about doing throughout the day.

She just needed to check out the rest of her house first.

Rebecca took a step toward the stairway and froze as her senses tingled again.

Had that been a squeak above her? Was it the floor upstairs crying out under unexpected weight?

The chills running through her became stronger. Rebecca didn't know what was going on, but she didn't like it.

On second thought, she couldn't take this chance.

She needed to get out of here. She wouldn't do anything to put her baby at risk.

Rebecca grabbed her purse from the entryway table and started to open the door. As she did, she looked back.

A man in a black mask stood at the top of her stairs, his hands clenched to his sides.

She let out a blood-curdling scream as fear consumed her.

She should have gotten out while she had the chance.

LEVI STONEMAN GRABBED two bags of groceries from the backseat of his car before slamming the door. He paused. A light rain pelted his black jacket, but he didn't care. Instead, he breathed in the fresh air here on Lantern Beach.

He had no idea this island would feel so refreshing. But something about the place and its saltwater-tinged air helped put him at ease. It had been a long time since he'd felt he could breathe.

He shifted the groceries in his arms. If he were honest with himself, he was tired of being on edge. Tired of his job and the constant clandestine assignments. He was ready to move on and live a normal life. But he'd come here for one last undercover assignment.

This job left him feeling like no one really knew him. He never stayed in one place long enough.

Never used the same identity. Instead, he'd hidden who he really was so deep inside himself Levi himself could hardly remember that person.

It hadn't bothered him until recently. Now a resounding loneliness pervaded his thoughts.

Levi's gaze wandered across his yard to his neighbor's house. Weathered cedar shingles, two stories with a porch, and five steps leading there.

He'd seen his neighbor leave this morning. She was blonde and pretty—and pregnant. He'd done his research and knew Rebecca Jarvis lived alone.

Just then, a scream sliced through the air. The sound came from next door.

The groceries slipped from Levi's arms. His boots dug into the sandy ground beneath him as he rushed between their houses. Without bothering to knock, he threw open the door.

His neighbor was on the floor, leaning against the wall and holding her belly—her very pregnant belly. Levi quickly scanned the house.

Seeing nothing threatening, he rushed toward the woman. Trembles had claimed her body, and tears flowed down her cheeks.

"Are you okay?" Levi knelt beside her, quickly assessing her for any injuries. He saw none.

She pointed toward the back of the house.

"There was a man. Here. In my house."

His muscles tensed as he followed her gaze. "Where did he go?"

"He shoved me down and ran out the back door."

Levi had only a second to make a decision. Follow the man or help his neighbor?

It didn't require much thought. His neighbor needed his attention more. Being injured while in her current state could be serious.

He pulled his phone from his pocket. "I'm going to call 911. You should be checked out."

She didn't argue with him. But more silent tears ran down her cheeks, and she rubbed her stomach, obviously worried about her baby.

After speaking with the dispatcher, Levi put his phone back into his pocket and turned to the woman. His gut twisted at the sight of her, followed by a flash of guilt. He shoved those emotions aside and slipped an arm behind her.

"Why don't we get you to the couch?"

She nodded, and Levi helped her stand. He didn't let go until she was seated on the navy-blue cushions. He sat a comfortable distance away and observed the woman again. Though she was clearly upset, he saw no wounds, no blood, nothing broken.

But he knew that didn't tell the whole story. "I'm

going to stay here with you until the ambulance arrives. Does anything hurt?"

"I think I'm okay. Just shaken."

Levi tried to picture what had happened. "He shoved you, you said?"

"That's right. He grabbed me, and I fought back. I knew I couldn't go anywhere with him. I think he was going to force me outside when he heard you at the door. He pushed me down and ran."

"Thank goodness I got here when I did." But Levi would be lying if he didn't admit that the whole scenario bothered him. Why would someone be hiding in this woman's house? The fact that she was pregnant made her even more vulnerable.

"I'm Levi Stoneman, by the way. I'm staying next door."

"I'm Rebecca Jarvis." She rubbed her belly. "I just hope my baby is okay. She's not moving a lot right now."

"She?"

Her lip twitched, a slight smile forming. "That's right. I'm having a girl. I'm going to name her Emma."

"Emma is a nice name."

"It was my grandma's name."

Just then, a siren sounded in the distance. The

sound became louder until finally it stopped outside the house.

Help was here.

But this wasn't the way Levi had intended on meeting Rebecca Jarvis or starting his investigation on her.

CHAPTER TWO

"YOU'RE GOING to be fine, Rebecca." Doc Clemson lowered his stethoscope. "You and your baby too."

Relief filled Rebecca, and she rubbed her stomach. Almost as if Emma understood what the doctor said, the baby kicked Rebecca's side. Normally, Rebecca might squirm with discomfort, but she was so happy to know everything was okay that she didn't care.

Just like she didn't care, at the moment, about the pungently clean scent here at the clinic. Or about beeps coming from across the hall. Or the hushed dialogue of nurses as they spoke outside the room.

She'd never liked hospitals, and this clinic seemed like one. Hospitals only brought bad memories. When her baby came, she hoped all that would change.

"She's running out of room in there, isn't she?" Doc Clemson raised his eyebrows, his ruddy complexion and orange-yellow hair forming a personable picture. The man could be a jokester, but he was also very good at his job. The island was lucky to have him.

Rebecca nodded, remembering her recent aches and pains. Emma appeared to be using her kidney as a pillow, and the babe's favorite thing to do was to kick her mama in the ribs. "Yes, she's a little crowded. Only three more weeks until she makes her grand entrance into the world."

Doc Clemson stepped back. He was like a father figure to people in this area. Rebecca could use a father figure now, especially considering everything that had happened in her life over the past seven months. He'd been a good sounding board throughout it all.

"How are you doing, Rebecca?" Doc Clemson peered at her over the top of his glasses. "How are you *really* doing?"

She shrugged, a rock forming in her chest. She didn't know how to answer that question . . . going into this pregnancy alone, having her husband abandon her, then die, trying to make ends meet. It hadn't been a walk in the park. Then mix in what had happened today . . . but the last thing she wanted was for people to feel sorry for her.

"I guess I'm doing as well as can be expected. I never thought I would be a single mom, but sometimes you just have to take what life hands you and make the best of it."

"Having a good attitude can go a long way." Doc Clemson jotted a note and then put his pen back into his front pocket. "But, remember, we're all here for you if you need us."

After several months of mounting problems, her husband, Jim, had left her. A month later, he'd died in a freak accident when someone tried to rob him in a parking lot. The altercation turned ugly, and the man had shot him. Police still hadn't caught the man responsible.

Rebecca had mourned his passing, but maybe she hadn't mourned it as she should. Guilt plagued her at that thought. She and Jim had been drifting apart for a while. Though she had been determined to make her marriage work, there was no denying the damage that had already been done.

She figured the sooner she accepted her new reality, the better it would be for her and Emma in the future. A lot of good people had stepped in to help her out. Rebecca wouldn't trade this community for anything.

She slid down from the exam table and took a moment to catch her balance. She was all stomach, and sometimes the disproportionate weight in her belly made her wobble.

Doc Clemson caught her elbow. "I'll walk you out."

Rebecca didn't argue. They strolled down the hallway of the island's clinic, Doc Clemson in no hurry. She didn't complain—she didn't move as fast as she used to.

"Any special plans for this week?" he asked.

"I'm showing a couple of houses, and . . ." She glanced at her watch. "It looks like I'll still be able to make my meeting with Patrick Peterson."

"Insurance stuff, huh?"

"Yes. It's taking forever to try to get my affairs in order after Jim's death."

Clemson squeezed her elbow before pushing the door open. "I'm sorry to hear about that."

Outside, a blustery wind and light precipitation surrounded them. The doc walked her to her small SUV. The police chief had one of her officers leave it there for Rebecca.

"Thank you, Doc." Rebecca offered a grateful smile. "For everything."

He was a good man. Not many people could say their general practitioner was also their obstetrician and the town coroner. It made for some interesting conversations.

Clemson offered one more wave before disappearing inside.

With another surge of gratefulness rushing through her, Rebecca climbed into her vehicle. She had just enough time to make her appointment.

But when she remembered the man who'd been in her house, a cold wash of fear spread through her. She glanced around the parking lot.

What if that man was watching her now? What if he wasn't finished with her yet?

Nausea gurgled in her stomach at the thought.

"SO, you haven't seen anything strange or unusual?"

Levi observed Police Chief Cassidy Chambers as she stood in front of him with a pad of paper and pen in hand. They were outside Rebecca's house, standing on the small porch. The chief had offered for them to sit in her car, but Levi had insisted he'd be fine out here.

He'd done his research on the chief before coming to Lantern Beach. Knowing the facts before entering a situation was the best way to prepare and not be caught by surprise. The attribute had served him well throughout his career.

"No, I haven't seen anything out of the ordinary," he told her. "Then again, I just got here yesterday evening. I'm not sure I know what strange and unusual is on this island yet."

"I can assure you that there is a lot of strange and unusual in this area," the police chief said dryly. "You'll learn that soon enough. We take incidents like what happened today very seriously."

"I'm glad she wasn't hurt." He paused and leaned against a post, careful to stay out of the steady rain that thrummed around them. "Have you heard any updates? I know it's not my business but . . ."

"I just called Rebecca. She said she and the baby are doing fine."

His shoulders softened with relief. "I'm glad to hear that."

Even though Levi was here to do a job, he would never wish harm on anyone—especially not a pregnant woman. He'd never forget the look on Rebecca's face when he'd found her on the floor holding her stomach.

Despite her seeming vulnerability, he needed to keep his eyes wide open. Even the most innocent person could be the mastermind of a criminal operation. He knew that firsthand.

"If you see anything . . ." Chief Chambers put her pad and pen back into her pocket before looking up at him, her eyes assessing.

The woman was smart and astute. Levi needed to keep that in mind.

"I'll definitely keep my eyes open," Levi said. "You'll be the first person I call."

"Thanks. We like to look out for each other around here. Rebecca has lived on this island for a long time, and we're all very protective of her, especially in her current state."

"Neighbors looking after neighbors?" Levi said. "It sounds like I'm going to like it in Lantern Beach."

"I hope you do."

He watched the chief as she walked back to her car. The woman seemed competent enough, and she had a great track record for solving crime in this town.

But Levi had come here for a purpose, and he couldn't let himself lose focus.

This wasn't the way he'd planned on starting his assignment. But it had been the perfect way to gain Rebecca's trust.

Why did guilt fill him at that thought?

One last job, he reminded himself. One last job.

But he already knew this assignment would be different than most.

CHAPTER THREE

"JUST GET me that information as soon as you can," Patrick called, standing in the doorway of his office as Rebecca departed. The man with his light-wash jeans, long-sleeved polo, and soft voice was about as boring as all the forms Rebecca had just read over.

Poor guy . . . it wasn't his fault. His job was just awful. Rebecca dreaded each time she had to meet with him.

"I'll do that." Rebecca waved as she stepped out of his office and headed toward her SUV. "Thanks for your help today."

"No problem, Mrs. Jarvis. And Merry Christmas!"

That was right. The holiday was three weeks

away. Rebecca would probably talk to him again before then. But she still couldn't believe how quickly time had flown by. Emma would be here soon.

She still needed a couple more sales to pad her bank account before winter hibernation fully set in.

Rebecca pulled her coat closer as a cool wind swept over the island. Living here in the summer was like being in paradise. But living here in the winter was like residing in an ice box. When the breeze came over the ocean, it was like nature had cranked the AC to preserve the locals until tourist season started again.

Despite that, there was still no place she would rather be.

The meeting with Patrick had felt stressful. Nobody wanted to think about wills, life insurance, and all the things that accompanied death. Even her husband's final arrangements had felt awkward.

Rebecca had Jim's body cremated, and then, while standing on the seashore, she and several friends had said a few things about him before releasing his ashes into the ocean.

It hadn't been especially beautiful, nor had it been especially sad. Too much had happened between them for the moment to bring the agony it deserved.

More guilt hit Rebecca at that thought. Jim had been her husband. He deserved someone who would mourn more for him. But he'd caused her so much hurt that it was difficult for Rebecca to truly grieve him the way she felt she should.

She climbed in her SUV and headed toward her place. As she did, she glanced in her rearview mirror. Why did she still feel like someone was watching her?

Rebecca sucked in a breath when she saw a black sedan appear in her rearview mirror. The car had tinted windows and remained a steady distance behind her.

She glanced back at the road in front of her and jerked the wheel, trying to stay between the lines.

Concentrate, Rebecca. Concentrate.

But her hands felt sweaty on the steering wheel. What if that was her attacker behind her? What if he planned on finishing what he'd started?

She swallowed hard.

She couldn't drive like this for much longer. It wasn't safe. Her concentration was shot.

Only a few more minutes, and you'll be back at your house, she told herself.

She glanced behind her one more time.

The car turned.

Rebecca released the air in her lungs. She was just being paranoid. She *had* to get a grip.

Finally, she pulled into her driveway. She sat there for a moment, trying to compose herself. She glanced into the seat beside her and saw the apple rhubarb pie. She'd had a few minutes before her appointment with Patrick, so she'd swung by one of her favorite restaurants, The Crazy Chefette, and had picked up the dessert.

It had seemed so normal—too normal—considering everything that had happened today.

She sucked in one more long breath before exiting her SUV. Gripping the pie in her hands, she climbed the steps to her neighbor's place. As a realtor, she knew the cottage was only a rental. That most likely meant that Levi wouldn't be staying for a long time. Still, Rebecca was grateful for his help today.

After another moment of hesitation, Rebecca knocked on the door. A few seconds later, the man pulled his door open, his eyes lighting with surprise.

Her breath caught at the sight of him. She vaguely remembered what Levi looked like from earlier, but seeing him now reminded her how handsome he was. The man was on the taller side, with dark hair and a dark beard. It wasn't the messy, scraggly kind of beard she often saw around here. But instead his facial hair looked neat, clean, and well-kept.

As did this man. There didn't appear to be an ounce of fat on his lean, sculpted body. He didn't flaunt his muscles like some men might. Instead, he wore jeans and a long-sleeved green shirt that was just loose enough to conceal his well-cared-for build.

Not that any of that mattered. At eight months pregnant, Rebecca wasn't looking for love or romance or even a fling. She had enough on her plate as it was.

A soft smile formed on his lips, and he opened the door wider. "Rebecca. I wasn't expecting to see you here."

She held up the neatly boxed pie. "I just wanted to bring you something to say thanks."

As Rebecca handed him the dessert, Levi took it from her and glanced through the cellophane top. "A pie? This looks great. But you didn't have to do that."

"I wanted to," Rebecca said. "If you hadn't shown up today when you did . . . I don't know that I would be here right now or that my precious Emma would be okay. This is the least I could do."

"I appreciate the gesture." He leaned against the door frame. "How are you doing?"

She nodded, feeling a strange rush of sentiment. Pregnancy and the heightened emotions that came with it made her feel off-balance. She wasn't normally prone to crying easily, but all that had changed lately.

"I'm doing okay." She swiped a hair behind her ear. "Thank you."

He paused, his blue eyes seemed full of both concern and curiosity. "Look, I know this might sound weird, but would you like to join me for a piece of this pie?"

Rebecca hesitated. Normally, she would say no. She didn't know this man. But the thought of eating a slice of that pie made her stomach grumble. Her cravings had been off the charts lately. And this man had saved her life, so he didn't appear to be a threat.

Unlike that other man.

She glanced at her house and shivered. She almost hated the thought of stepping foot inside there again. Would she ever feel safe at home again?

She didn't know.

She thought about Levi's offer only a moment

longer and then nodded. "Maybe I will take a piece of pie. Pie makes everything better, correct?"

"Makes perfect sense to me." Levi flashed another soft smile.

Seeing the kind look on his face reassured her. Rebecca stepped inside his house and hoped she didn't regret this.

But until she knew who that man in her house had been, she'd be on guard. She'd be foolish not to be.

LEVI SLICED into the pie and put two pieces on white plates. As he did, he glanced out the window. He'd seen the same dark sedan drive by three times since the incident at Rebecca's place. Who was in the driver's seat?

He didn't know, and he didn't like it.

But Levi couldn't show Rebecca how edgy he felt. It would look suspicious—especially when she found out he was supposed to be an engineer. Too bad acting classes hadn't been part of his studies at Quantico.

Seeing Rebecca at his doorstep had been a surprise. He had to admit that it felt fortuitous.

What better way to get to know Rebecca than by sharing some dessert together?

Levi didn't want to think that she might be involved in anything illegal, but he needed to find out. It was what he'd been sent here to do. But he couldn't let her know that. His boss didn't believe that was the best way to proceed.

"So what brings you this way?" Rebecca sat at the kitchen table behind him, sipping a warm cup of apple cider.

He swallowed a burst of remorse and remembered his cover story. "I needed a place to get away to for a while. I work from home, and my neighbor used to always talk about coming to Lantern Beach as a child. He talked about it so much that I knew I had to see it for myself. Besides, you can get great rental rates around here in the off-season."

"Yes, you can. Some people really love the quiet here on the island in the winter. It helps them relax. And locals . . . they like it because they can recover after our crazy summers."

He set a piece of pie in front of her before lowering himself into the chair across the table. "I've heard this is quite the destination when it's warm. If you don't mind me asking, how long have you lived here?"

"My family has a lot of history in the area, actually." Rebecca picked up her fork. "My dad was a fisherman here, and his dad was a fisherman before him."

"I'd say you do have a lot of history here then. Does your dad still work as a fisherman?" He glanced outside again, looking for any sign of trouble. Everything looked clear.

"He moved from being a fisherman to owning a seafood processing facility. He retired three years ago. Then my mom passed, and he decided to head down to Florida. He actually met someone online." Her voice trailed, and Levi could sense some tension.

"Wow."

"Yeah, wow. But she seems nice. Anyway, my brothers and sister left the island also. I'm the only one who ended up staying." She took a dainty bite of the pie.

"You must really like it here then."

"Lantern Beach is home to me. I can't imagine leaving. Besides, this is where my business is. There's nothing I love more than helping people find their dream homes here on the island. I want them to have a little bit of the peace and contentment that I have living here."

Her words sounded so sincere that she nearly

sold Levi on settling down here too. But his life was back in Philadelphia. Up there, he never had a dull moment. Life was fast-paced. Sure, he may not be able to hear the ocean from his house, but he *could* hear a nearby interstate.

He frowned. It wasn't quite the same. As he remembered life back home, his lungs tightened, and he longed for another whiff of fresh air. Instead, he remembered his mission here.

"I've been considering buying a second home." He took a bite of his pie, and the sweet and tart flavor washed over his taste buds. "Maybe this will be the place to look at doing that."

Levi had rehearsed that idea, and he knew it was his best opportunity to get to know Rebecca better.

He shoved aside his guilt at the thought. It used to be so easy for him to do this job, to use various methods to find out the information he needed. But it was becoming harder and harder lately.

"I could show you a few places that have great rental income histories." Rebecca's gaze brightened. "If you're interested."

"I just might take you up on that." Levi shifted as his thoughts turned over.

He'd come here with only one goal in mind—finding out if Rebecca Jarvis was also involved in her husband's weapons-smuggling operation. They needed to know names, times, details.

Rebecca might just be the person to give him that information.

Records showed that Jim Jarvis had banked a large sum of money before his death. Levi felt certain Rebecca had that money now.

This operation was delicate, not the kind that required interrogations. Rather, he needed more creative ways of finding answers.

But what if Rebecca was a victim in this instead of an accomplice?

He stored the question away.

Their conversation had been pleasant, and he hated to ruin it. But he didn't have time to remain superficial—not when so much was on the line. "Rebecca, I know this is none of my business. But do you have any idea why someone was in your house earlier today? I haven't been able to stop thinking about it."

Her smile slipped, and she lowered her fork back onto her plate. Instantly, Levi regretted asking the question. But he had a job to do. He had to keep that in mind. As easy as the conversation felt and as pleasant as Rebecca was to be around, Levi couldn't lose sight of his reason for being here.

"I have no idea. I live a pretty boring life. I can't imagine why anyone would want to break into my place."

Levi wanted to ask her about her baby's father. He knew the answers. He knew all about what had happened to Jim. But he wanted to hear her perspective. However, Levi didn't feel like they were at the point where he could ask for something so personal without raising suspicions.

Rebecca took her last bite of pie and pushed her plate away. "Thank you so much for sharing the pie with me. But I really should be going now."

He stood also. "No, I should be thanking you. And I think I will take you up on that offer to see some houses. Just let me know what works with your schedule."

"I actually have some time tomorrow." She picked up her purse from the floor beside her, pulled out a business card, and handed it to him.

"Tomorrow would be perfect."

She copied his smile. "I'll set some things up for you in the morning then. How about if we meet at 10:30?"

"Sounds great."

Levi walked Rebecca to the door and watched as

she walked across the lawn to her house. This was going to be an interesting assignment.

He glanced at the street one more time. He hadn't seen the car lately. But that didn't mean the man driving it was gone.

Concern twisted in his gut at the thought.

He'd keep an eye on things . . . he couldn't afford not to.

CHAPTER FOUR

THE NEXT MORNING, Rebecca looked in the bathroom mirror and flinched when she saw the circles under her eyes.

She'd hardly gotten any sleep last night. She'd kept waiting to hear the floor creak. To see clandestine movement. To feel pain.

She'd gotten up several times to check the doors and windows. She'd even peered outside, looking for any strange visitors.

Rebecca had seen no one.

As she padded downstairs and into the kitchen, her questions remained.

Why had someone been in her house yesterday? Did they think she had something of value in the house? If so, they had to be sorely disappointed.

Mostly, she had knickknacks from her childhood and heirlooms that had been passed down to her through the generations.

She yawned and poured herself a cup of coffee. Only one cup a day. That's what the doctor said she could have, and she was careful not to go beyond that.

She'd taken to drinking warm water for the rest of the day. The liquid gave her the illusion of coffee without the taste and without the caffeine. It was a small sacrifice to keep her baby healthy.

As Rebecca's phone buzzed, she glanced at her screen. A message from her bank popped up. Her eyes widened. Her account was overdrawn.

"What . . . ?" she muttered.

She set her mug down and grabbed her laptop. Quickly, she logged into her bank. She sucked in a breath when she saw her account balance was two hundred dollars in the red. How was that possible?

As she scanned the recent transactions, a sick feeling formed in her gut.

She hadn't made these withdrawals.

Rebecca sagged against the table. Why this? Why now?

She was going to be on the phone with the bank all morning trying to get this straightened out. She'd been looking forward to taking it easy for an hour or two before showing Levi some homes.

With a sigh, she began making phone calls.

Two hours later, Rebecca pulled her coat on. She'd told Levi she would show him some houses at eleven, and she couldn't afford to cancel.

The bank had told her they'd opened a claim and would get back with her. In the meantime, they'd given her a temporary credit and canceled her debit card. What awful timing.

She shoved those thoughts aside. More than ever, she needed to make another sale.

Then again, Rebecca reminded herself, she did have some money coming in, thanks to Jim's life insurance policy. She just needed to get a copy of his death certificate to Patrick today. She hadn't realized just how involved all of this would be.

Normally, it would only take around a month to get a payout, but she hadn't realized this policy even existed until she got a letter in the mail about it.

Grabbing her purse and briefcase, Rebecca stepped outside. Just as yesterday, the brisk wind that swept over the landscape chilled her down to the bones. Her internal thermostat was completely berserk. One minute, she was having a hot flash, and the next instant she felt freezing cold.

As she started across the sandy lawn to meet Levi, his door opened and he stepped out. A flutter rushed through her. Why in the world would she have that reaction?

She ran a hand through her hair. There was no good reason. She just needed to ignore the feeling and remain professional.

"Good morning," she called, hiking her purse strap up higher on her shoulder. "Are you ready to go?"

He straightened the dark blue scarf around his neck. "As a matter of fact, I am. The more I thought about this last night, the more I'm intrigued by the possibility of finding a place here."

"If you're looking for an investment opportunity, Lantern Beach is a great place."

They stepped toward her vehicle, and Rebecca's keys jangled in her hands.

"Listen, how do you feel about me driving?" Levi paused before they crossed the lawn. "You seem like you could use a load off your feet, and I don't mind."

Rebecca started to respond when a vehicle driving past caught her attention. Was that the same car that had followed her yesterday? Her lungs tightened at the thought.

"Everything okay?" Levi studied her.

Rebecca nodded, even though she wasn't sure if everything was okay or not. She was probably being paranoid. It probably went back to those pregnancy hormones. They made everything seem heightened.

The car sped up as it went past, but the tinted windows didn't allow her to see inside. Levi followed her gaze and squinted.

"You know that driver?" he asked.

She snapped her head back toward him, realizing that she was entirely too easy to read. "No, I have no idea who that was. Sorry. I guess I'm just on edge after everything that happened yesterday."

He tilted his head. "You didn't have any more trouble last night, did you?"

The concern in Levi's voice caused warmth to flare through her. "No, no trouble. I only had some difficulty sleeping. I kept anticipating trouble that never came."

"That seems perfectly normal considering what happened."

Rebecca stared at him another moment, the sincerity in his voice winning her trust. Having him next door seemed to be an answer to prayer.

At that moment, her phone beeped. She looked down at her screen and felt her head spin.

"Rebecca?"

She pulled her gaze away from her phone and frowned. But all she could think about were the words she'd read there.

You have something that belongs to me, and I intend to get it back—no matter the cost.

Who was targeting her? And why?

LEVI DIDN'T like the way things were going so far.

He'd come here to see if Rebecca was complicit in the illegal affairs of her husband. It was becoming clear that she wasn't. The break-in yesterday followed by the mysterious car today all pointed to a different scenario than the one Levi initially had in mind.

What had been in that text? She looked white as a ghost after she'd read it.

Despite that, the morning was going well— surprisingly well, for that matter. Rebecca had shown him four different houses. Two of them seemed to be really good possibilities.

Rebecca had proven she knew what she was doing when it came to real estate. She spoke with knowledge and insight as she'd answered all his questions. Even though Levi hadn't really come to

Lantern Beach with the intention of buying a rental property, she'd made a convincing case.

What would it be like to start over in a place like this? To leave his high-stress job behind?

His career had consumed his life for the past five years. He'd welcomed the distraction, at first. It seemed like a better option than remembering Brianna's betrayal.

A thud echoed inside him at the thought, reminding him of the emptiness he'd been fighting. This wasn't the way he'd envisioned his life turning out, but he'd tried to make the best of it. That was fine . . . until he would get glimpses of what he was missing.

What had caused that thought? Lantern Beach? Rebecca? He wasn't sure. But if he was smart, he'd forget about it.

"So what do you think?" Rebecca asked as they paused inside the last house.

It was a small ocean-front bungalow that had been recently updated. The place would require hardly any renovations. Levi had to admit the property was intriguing.

"I would say that Lantern Beach is a great place." He craned his neck and nodded at the high ceilings strapped with weathered wooden beams. "You've definitely given me a lot to think about."

As he said the words, Rebecca leaned against the doorframe and closed her eyes. Though she'd been trying not to show it, Levi could tell she was tired. When she thought Levi wasn't looking, Rebecca rubbed her back and shifted uncomfortably.

She shouldn't be working now. She was far enough along in her pregnancy that she deserved to have some time to relax and nest.

Levi frowned. That wasn't the hand that life dealt her. As a single mom, no doubt she needed to get all the work she could. She'd been programmed with that survival instinct.

"Just let me know if you would like to make an offer on anything." Rebecca handed him some proformas that listed projected rental calculations on each of the houses. "Obviously, you know where to find me."

He smiled, catching a whiff of Rebecca's flowery perfume as she leaned closer. "Yes, I'm lucky that I happened to pick a rental right beside a real estate agent. You seem to really know the area."

"I meant it earlier when I said I love helping people find the home where they can grow in their dreams." As she said the words, her voice faded with a touch of wistfulness.

What was it about this woman that tugged on Levi's heartstrings? That wasn't a good sign. He needed to make sure his emotions weren't tangled in this.

If Rebecca was involved with her husband's illegal activities, she deserved to pay the penalty for it. This operation had cost too many innocent lives. A sweet disposition didn't equal innocence. He knew that firsthand.

"It looks like you could sit down for a while." He touched her elbow. "Why don't I get you back to your house?"

"Don't mind me." She waved him off. "I'm good to go."

Though she said the words, Levi didn't believe her.

They stepped out onto the deck to head back to his car. Levi took Rebecca's arm to help her down to the sidewalk, afraid she might lose her balance. As they slowly made their way down the steps, his gaze drifted.

A dark sedan slowly drove by on the street. Levi's gut tightened. It was the same car from earlier. Someone was definitely watching her.

He glanced at the license plate, but sand covered it.

The thought of someone going to such extreme measures caused a shot of anger to rush through him. It appeared that Rebecca and her baby were in danger. Levi couldn't let anything happen to them. But how was he going to protect them when Rebecca was a mere stranger?

He tucked her into his car before climbing in himself. As he took off, Levi looked in his mirror. The sedan appeared. Something about the vehicle put him on edge—especially as it gained speed on them.

"What's going on?" Rebecca asked.

Levi wanted to assure her it was nothing. But he couldn't.

The car was on his bumper now.

He pressed the gas pedal. "Hold on."

"What?" Rebecca's voice sounded breathless.

"I'm sorry. But I think this driver is going to ram us."

CHAPTER FIVE

REBECCA CLOSED her eyes and began lifting fervent prayers.

Why was this happening? Why did someone keep coming after her?

"Try to relax," Levi coached.

Relax? That was the last thing on her mind.

He pressed the accelerator even harder, and his car zoomed down the highway.

Rebecca knew she shouldn't, but she glanced behind her.

She saw the same dark sedan she'd seen earlier. It was back.

And this time the driver wasn't being shy.

"You ever seen that car before?" Levi asked, his hand white-knuckled on the steering wheel.

"I thought the driver was following me yesterday."

"I thought I saw it drive past your house earlier also." He continued to fly down the highway. Thankfully, no one else was out here.

"You did?"

Levi nodded, his neck appearing stiff. "I did. This guy isn't backing off. We're going to need to figure out a way to lose him. Any ideas?"

Rebecca's mind raced. How did they lose someone who wanted to ram into them? She had no clue. There weren't even any stoplights on the island.

Unless . . .

"Head to the lighthouse," she rushed.

"The lighthouse? Isn't that a dead end?"

"Trust me."

He glanced at her again before nodding. "Okay then."

He pressed the accelerator harder, afraid the car would ram them.

Rebecca's hand went to her stomach. Emma, Emma, Emma . . . she had to protect Emma.

But the situation right now felt hopeless.

If only they could make it to the lighthouse. It wasn't too much farther away. Maybe one mile.

"Can you speed up?" she asked.

Levi glanced at her again. "Are you sure?"

"I'm sure."

"Okay."

LEVI PRESSED the accelerator even harder, knowing he was close to maxing out at the vehicle's top speed. He wanted to get away from the driver behind them . . . but he also needed to be safe.

The balance was delicate. He'd had many defensive driving classes. However, with Rebecca being pregnant, everything felt more complicated.

He had no idea what her plan was. But he hoped it was a good one. He was going to have to trust her, something he wasn't good at doing.

Finally, he'd put enough distance between them and the car that he could breathe easier—but only for a minute.

The road curved ever so slightly as they entered a wooded area surrounding the lighthouse.

The tension in his back returned.

Rebecca glanced over her shoulder and then looked back at him. "Turn here. Now!"

He braked as he jerked the wheel to the left, and his car barreled through some underbrush. As soon as the foliage disappeared, a gravel path appeared.

"Keep going!" Rebecca said.

He did as she said, only stopping as the path ended at the water.

He sucked in several deep breaths as he realized what had just happened.

"No one knows this road is here," Rebecca rubbed her arms, as if chilled. "It's a locals only type of thing."

"I can see why. It's beautiful here."

Rebecca nodded but glanced behind her again. "I don't think the other driver saw us."

"I don't think he did either. But let's wait a few minutes, okay?"

She nodded.

Levi reached over and squeezed her hand, trying to put her at ease. "Good job."

"Thank you."

They waited ten minutes before Levi turned around and headed back toward the highway. Tension snaked through him as he anticipated the other car waiting there for them. He prayed that wasn't the case.

As he reached the street, he saw it was clear.

With a deep sigh of relief, he pulled onto the highway and headed back.

"How did you know how to drive like that?" Rebecca glanced at him, and he could feel her gaze burning into him.

Levi shrugged. He'd wondered if she might ask that question. "I just followed my instincts."

"I'm glad you have good instincts then."

He offered a quick, sad smile. "Me too."

"I'm going to need to report this." She pulled out her phone, dialed a number, and recited what had happened to the person on the other end. When she ended the call, she turned toward Levi. "The police are going to look into it."

"Hopefully, they'll be able to track down the driver," Levi said.

"I hope so. Because whoever is doing this needs to be caught before something more serious happens."

Levi glanced at her, curiosity brimming inside him. "You have no idea why someone could be doing this?"

"I have no idea." Her voice cracked, but, as her gaze fell on a sign in the distance, her eyes narrowed.

He followed her eyes and saw an advertisement for the town Christmas parade. "You don't like the parade?"

She shook her head, seeming to come out of her stupor. "The parade? I do like the parade. Sorry. It's just that it's sponsored by Jared Nicholson."

"And that's a problem?"

"He's a new realtor in town. I'd like to say that I'm not feeling threatened, but I am."

"Threatened?"

"Not physically. I should clarify that after everything that's happened. Just my business. There are only so many houses to sell here on the island."

"I suppose that's true." Levi glanced at her again, realizing that they both needed to decompress after what had happened. "Listen, I know we're both still reeling from that car chase. Maybe it would be good for both of our nerves to get something to eat. What do you think?"

Rebecca opened her eyes and raised her head long enough to glance at him. He knew she was trying to feel him out. Trying to ascertain what his intentions were.

"No pressure," he added. "But I don't know anyone else in town, so it would be nice to have some company. Plus, I may have some more real estate questions."

That last sentence seemed to set her at ease, and she nodded. "Sure, I know just the place where we can eat."

CHAPTER SIX

REBECCA DIRECTED Levi to The Crazy Chefette. It was her favorite restaurant on the island, and the owner, Lisa Dillinger, and her husband, Braden, were kind souls.

Whenever Rebecca came in, she felt like she was at her mom's kitchen table. Plus, in the winter months when it was mostly locals in town, this was a great community gathering place where everyone caught up with each other.

Now that her husband was gone, Rebecca had been reminded about the importance of community and making sure she was a part of it. She didn't know what she would have done during these recent months without her friends here on Lantern Beach as well as her church family.

57

A shiver raked through her as she remembered that car chasing them. It all seemed surreal, almost like a dream instead of reality. Why would someone be going to such extremes? It just didn't make sense.

She tried to push those thoughts aside.

"So what do you recommend here?" Levi skimmed the menu, but Rebecca noticed that he occasionally glanced up as if trying to gauge her mental state.

"Lisa is known for her grilled cheese and peach sandwiches. I realize they're not for everyone, but I think they are delicious and tasty. She also makes some excellent homemade chips. But anything you find on the menu will be good."

Levi made a face. "Grilled cheese and peach sandwiches, huh? I don't think I've ever heard of that combination before."

"I hadn't either, but once I tried it, I was addicted. It's my new favorite."

He closed his menu, his eyes sparkling. "Then I'm sold. I have to try it while I'm in town."

Just then, Lisa came by with a pad of paper in hand, a smile on her face, and her blonde hair as bouncy as ever. "Rebecca, how's that baby doing?"

"Emma is doing great." Rebecca felt herself

glowing as she said the words. "She's ready to make her grand entrance soon."

"I know. We are all excited to meet her." Lisa turned to Levi and extended her hand. "Hi, I'm Lisa."

"I'm Levi." Levi shook her hand in return before glancing around the restaurant. "Looks like a great place you have here."

"Thanks. I like it."

They ordered their food. Before they could begin a conversation again, someone else approached the table.

Ron Davis.

Jim's former boss.

The man was small and thin, with a receding hairline and oversized glasses. Rebecca had always liked him, though, despite a bad history between him and her husband.

"Good to see you, Rebecca," Ron started.

She introduced him to Levi, and they chatted for a few minutes.

"How's business going?" Rebecca asked.

Ron shrugged. "I wish I could say well, but we've been struggling."

She tilted her head. "Struggling?"

"Tourism rates were down this year. You know what they say about businesses the size of mine.

We're going to have make-or-break years. This may be the one that breaks us."

"I'm so sorry to hear that."

As he walked away, a moment of silence fell between her and Levi. Her thoughts turned.

Was Ron's business struggling because of the missing money?

Before she caught herself, she frowned. Levi's eyes narrowed as he observed her.

Rebecca had to admit that there was something about Levi that made her feel like she had known him much longer than twenty-four hours. He was laid-back and easy to talk with. Plus, he was engaging and handsome to boot.

Jim had been more of the quiet, brooding type. Not that she was complaining. Rebecca had fallen in love with the man, after all. But years of being married and witnessing his mood swings had worn her down. She constantly felt like she was walking on eggshells.

He hadn't been a fan of her sentimental ways. He hated her old family house and heirlooms and chastised her for wanting to keep them. It had been refreshing to hear Levi say that he appreciated those things yesterday.

She tried to turn her mind away from the heavy thoughts.

"So," Rebecca took a sip of her hot water, "How long are you here for?"

Levi settled back and shrugged. "I'll probably be in town for the next month or so."

She raised her eyebrows. "That's a long time to stay. But at least you'll be here for the Christmas celebrations on Lantern Beach. We've got a tree lighting, carolers. It's a lot of fun."

He smiled. "I look forward to it then."

"What was it that you said you did again?"

"I'm an engineer." He raised a shoulder. "Exciting, right?"

"Sure," Rebecca said, looking unconvinced.

He laughed. "No, I don't suppose it is that exciting. But it is nice to be able to work remotely when necessary."

"I would imagine. Though I do like working for myself, there are moments when I think it would be nice to work for a corporation. To have that steady paycheck instead of relying on sales all the time."

"But I can see that you are really good at what you do. It's a blessing to be able to support yourself with your own business and set your own hours.

Plus, it has to be nice not to have a boss breathing down your neck."

"I suppose that what you're saying is true. I'm blessed, and I don't need to forget that."

She glanced outside and remembered the car that had chased them. She had tried to play it off like it hadn't affected her. She didn't want to see Levi become concerned, and she liked to think she could take care of herself, even though she knew she couldn't.

But that, when combined with the threatening text and the break-in yesterday, had her feeling entirely more nervous than she would like.

She didn't see anyone suspicious outside. She hoped it stayed that way. Maybe this was all just a fluke, and it would pass.

But her gut told her there was more to the story. Was it because of Jim? Had he done something before he died?

That was a question Rebecca wished she didn't have to ask herself. But she'd be a fool not to.

LEVI WATCHED REBECCA. She was still on edge, wasn't she? Anybody in their right mind would be shaken after what happened earlier. She seemed to be handling it surprisingly well. He could admire her for that.

They made general chitchat about the island until their food came. He then asked Rebecca if it was okay if he prayed over the meal. She said yes, and Levi offered thanks for the food. As he took a bite of his sandwich, the unusual combination of flavors washed over his taste buds.

He saw Rebecca watching his reaction and nodded. "This is good."

She smiled, as if pleased. "I'm glad you like it."

He picked up one of his chips and looked at her. She really was lovely, with her soft features and glowing skin. Even though she was pregnant, she was trim and her hair had a healthy sheen.

Not that her looks changed anything. He was still here to investigate her.

Levi shifted. "Look, I know this probably isn't my place, and you can tell me to shut up or leave you alone or whatever you need to say, and I wouldn't blame you. But, if you don't mind me asking, is your baby's father still in the picture?"

A gray cloud seemed to form over Rebecca's head, and she frowned. She placed her sandwich back onto her plate and licked her lips. "Actually, he died about six months ago."

"I'm sorry to hear that."

She hesitated again. "Thank you. But, before he died, we separated. Or, should I say, he left me. He was in a bad place in his life, and it spilled over into every area of our relationship. It's been a tough couple of years."

"I'm sorry to hear that. It sounds like you've been through a lot."

She picked up a chip and broke it in half but made no effort to eat it. "My husband used to work for one of the rental agencies in this area. He was accused of embezzling some money from it. He claimed he was innocent, and I believed him. His boss—Ron, whom you just met—didn't press charges but fired him instead. Despite that, Jim's reputation here on the island was ruined."

"That couldn't have been easy."

She continued to play with her chip. "No, it wasn't. He had trouble finding a new job. I became the breadwinner for the both of us. I tried to find things for Jim to do to pull him out of his melancholy state. Nothing I did seemed to work."

"Even knowing you were pregnant, he didn't try to turn things around?"

Levi knew he was probably treading in unwelcome territory. But he wanted to know, both professionally and personally.

"We had wanted a baby for years, but we were unable to have one," Rebecca said. "I thought it was going to be our lot in life to be childless. When I found out I was pregnant, I wondered if our marriage could be saved. Instead, he left me." Her voice cracked.

"And he didn't come back?" What an idiot. If Levi had a child, he would do anything to let the child know he or she was loved.

"He said something about making things right. But he died a couple weeks later. I guess he never had the chance to do that."

Levi had the urge to reach across the table, grab Rebecca's hand, and squeeze it. But it was too soon, too early. They didn't have that kind of relationship. Still, his heart went out to her after hearing what she'd been through.

"He was a fool to ever leave you," Levi said.

Rebecca's cheeks turned a subtle shade of pink. "Thank you. It hasn't been easy. Then again, we were never promised that life would be easy, were we?"

"No, we were not." No truer words had ever been spoken.

As they continued to eat, that sentiment remained on Levi's mind. No, life wasn't ever that easy. Levi knew that firsthand also. Unfortunately, life for Rebecca might get a lot harder before the storm subsided . . . if it subsided.

That all depended on her innocence.

CHAPTER SEVEN

REBECCA EXCUSED herself from the table to take a phone call from Cassidy.

She was happy for an excuse to get away from Levi for a minute—not because she wasn't enjoying his company. It was the opposite, actually. She was finding it entirely too easy to open up to the man.

Ordinarily, Rebecca wouldn't share so many personal details with a potential client. But Levi had asked about her husband, and maybe she just needed a listening ear. She'd certainly shared more than she'd planned.

It was nice to talk to someone who wasn't from the island. While everybody here had been kind and supportive, talking about Jim around people who'd known him for years seemed disrespectful.

Rebecca paused in the nook near the bathrooms. "Any leads?"

"No, not yet. We're trying to track down any dark sedans here on the island."

"Have you found any?"

Cassidy paused. "Let me ask you this. Have you had any beefs with Jared Nicholson?"

She sucked in a breath. "Jared? I mean, he's my competition but . . . I don't know I'd say we had problems. Does he have a dark sedan?"

"He does. I'm not saying he's behind this. Bradshaw went to talk to him. I'll let you know how that pans out."

"Thanks."

As she ended the call, Rebecca leaned against the wall for a minute. Jared couldn't be behind this . . . could he? She shivered at the thought.

Was all this about eliminating the competition? She hated to think that someone might take it that far. Then again, the few encounters she'd had with Jared had proven he was highly competitive. In fact, the first time they'd met he'd told her, "Prepare to be annihilated." He'd laughed afterward. Said he was joking.

But Rebecca still remembered the encounter, and a sour feeling turned in her stomach.

Plastering on a smile, Rebecca made her way back to the table where Levi was waiting for her. She reminded herself that she should remain more guarded. Levi would be leaving the island soon, so there was no need to form a connection with him.

She slipped into the booth, her belly barely fitting.

"Everything okay?" Levi's intelligent eyes stared back at her.

"Chief Chambers was just giving me an update on the sedan." She shared what the chief had told her.

Levi's expression remained unreadable. "Hopefully, she'll find some answers soon. But that seems like a pretty extreme reason to try to run you off the road."

"Real estate can be cutthroat, but you're right. I just can't see it." Unless there was more to the story than she realized . . .

Levi shifted, but his gaze still looked uneasy. "You have any more showings coming up?"

"As a matter of fact, I have a new client who would like to see some new houses tomorrow. We met last week."

Levi raised his eyebrows. "That has to make you happy."

"Yes, especially at this time of the year. It's unusual to have very many clients at all during these cold months."

"I guess if I'm going to make an offer on a house, I should really do it before you show it to someone else, huh?"

She grinned. "Competition always gets people moving faster."

She glanced at her phone as a text came in, and she frowned. Patrick was reminding her to get him the information for the life insurance.

"Good news followed by bad news?" Levi raised his eyebrows in curiosity.

"No, not bad news. I'm still trying to get my late husband's affairs in order. I found out he took out a big life insurance policy not long before he died. I had no idea he'd done so, but that must be what he meant when he said he would take care of us. However, I'm still trying to jump through legal loopholes so I can get the money."

Levi shifted. "It can be quite the process sometimes."

"Yes, it can be."

Rebecca noticed the subtle change in Levi's gaze. "What are you thinking?"

"You really want to know?" He raised his eyebrows, hesitation still written on his features.

"I do."

"You're getting a large payout. Do you think that has anything to do with the break-in or the car following you?"

She sucked in a quick breath. It was an excellent question. "I . . . I don't know. I didn't think about that, I guess."

Levi waved his hand in the air. "I'm sorry. I'm not trying to get you concerned. I'm just a solutions kind of guy. It's what I do."

The conversation suddenly made her feel uncomfortable, and doubt rooted itself in her mind. All of this had started before she went in to sign that paperwork . . .

"Listen, I should probably get back home." She grabbed her purse. "I do have some paperwork to do."

Levi nodded and stood. "I understand. I should get to work also."

But as Rebecca reached for her debit card, she remembered that it had been canceled.

LEVI READ Rebecca's face and knew he was pushing too hard. He needed to back off. However, hearing that information about the life insurance policy caused all kinds of red flags to go up in his mind.

From all appearances, Rebecca had no idea what her husband had been involved with. But Levi knew that the criminal enterprises Jim had gotten mixed up in had resulted in some large cash payouts. Now he feared the wrong people might want to get their hands on that money. Innocent or guilty, Rebecca was in danger either way.

Did this life insurance policy have something to do with everything that was going on? The timing was suspicious, so it wouldn't surprise him.

The more Levi learned, the more uncomfortable he was.

As they headed down the road back to their houses, Levi's mind raced.

Keep a placid expression, he reminded himself. He didn't want to alarm Rebecca. It wouldn't be good for her in her current state.

He glanced behind him in the rearview mirror but saw no one. At least that was good news.

"I think I'm going to have to go back and eat at

that restaurant again before I leave," Levi said, changing the subject into a more neutral area.

"I'm glad you liked it. I'm going to grab some cash at home and pay you back."

Her bank account had been compromised. Coincidence? Levi didn't think so. "Don't worry about it. I'm not."

"But you're my client."

"My mom always taught me I should never let a woman pay." Levi cast her a look, his eyes glimmering. "I know it sounds outdated now, but I still can't get those lessons or her voice out of my head."

Rebecca smiled, as if his answer had pleased her.

"That's a bummer about your bank account, though." Levi adjusted the heat until warm air blew through the vents. "Did that just happen?"

She nodded. "I just found out that my account had been compromised this morning."

"When it rains, it pours, huh?"

"You can say that again."

They pulled to a stop in her driveway, Levi threw the car into Park, and they stepped out. He would walk her to the door.

"You don't have to do this." Rebecca glanced at him, a frown forming on her lips. "I'm perfectly capable of getting to the door by myself."

"Yes, but this is something else my mama taught me."

She smiled again. He told the truth. His mother had raised him to be a gentleman.

As he took a step toward the front door, he paused, pulling Rebecca to a stop also. Her eyes jerked toward him in confusion.

"What—" she started.

"Rebecca, your front door is open. You didn't leave it that way, did you?"

The color left her face as she swung her gaze toward the front of the house. "No, I did not."

"I need you to go wait in my car. With the doors locked. Okay?" He only threw in the "okay" to soften his words. "And call 911."

Rebecca took a couple steps backward before reaching his car and climbing inside. Levi waited until he heard the door lock click before he proceeded. He needed to find out why that front door was open.

He had a bad feeling about this.

CHAPTER EIGHT

LEVI WAITED until he was inside the house and out of sight from Rebecca before pulling his gun. The Glock had been tucked away in an ankle holster all day. He hadn't wanted Rebecca to see it and begin asking questions. But he was glad that he had it now.

Cautiously, he moved against the interior wall and scanned the inside of Rebecca's house. The place had been ransacked—books strewn, wall hangings crooked, couch cushions scattered.

What in the world was someone looking for here? Levi didn't know, but he had a feeling it had something to do with Rebecca's former husband.

He paused near the stairway and listened.

Nothing.

If the intruder was still inside the house, he was being quiet. Hiding. Tucked out of sight.

None of those thoughts were comforting. Levi continued to move along the perimeter of the space, looking under everything and in every closet. The first floor was clear.

He moved up the stairs. The first bedroom was empty as well as the second.

He paused as he opened the last door. A lovely nursery stared back at him. The space had been decorated with an obvious amount of love and care. The walls were pink, a crib in the corner had a lovely angel-themed mobile over it. Light and airy curtains finished off the space, along with a rocking chair and matching rug.

The room was fit for a princess.

He frowned. Rebecca's little girl deserved every chance in life. All this stress at the end of Rebecca's pregnancy wasn't healthy, and seeing this nursery right now served as a grim reminder. But how could Levi keep them safe and investigate?

He wasn't sure, but he needed to figure out a way.

Satisfied that no one was here, Levi put his gun back into the holster. Just as he reached the downstairs, Chief Chambers stepped through the front door. He raised his hands, signaling he wasn't a threat.

With a frown, she paced toward him. "Did you see anything up there?"

"No, it appears clear."

She stared at him another moment before scanning the place. "Someone did a number here."

"Yes, they did."

"I guess it's a good thing that you were able to come to the rescue again."

Something about the way the chief said the words indicated that she was on to him. Levi was good at what he did. Good at covering up his true intentions. He had been doing it for a long time. So how was it that this woman was able to see through him?

He didn't know, and he didn't like it.

"Yes, I would say that it's a good thing that I just happened to be next door." He reminded himself not to carry himself like a soldier. He had to act like a civilian. Like an engineer.

Thankfully, his boss had thoroughly developed his new identity. Levi had a feeling the police chief would be looking into him.

"I'll take it from here." The chief's voice left no room for argument.

Levi stepped toward the front door, knowing he needed to back off. "Sounds like a plan. Is Rebecca still outside?"

"Yes, she is. I told her to remain in the car until we told her otherwise."

Levi nodded, an uneasy feeling still sloshing inside his gut. He couldn't ruin this. Not now. And not because he was letting his feelings get involved.

REBECCA WATCHED as Levi emerged from her home. Without waiting for a signal, she opened the door and rushed across the driveway toward him. Not even the cold wind slowed her down.

"Well?" Her mind had been racing through worst-case scenarios. Scenarios where Levi had ended up hurt or where something even more devastating happened.

Why would someone be doing this to her? Why was she being targeted? It made no sense. Her whole world felt rocked.

"Somebody went through your things. Only you

can say if anything is missing. I'm just glad you weren't home when this person came through."

Rebecca felt her shoulders hunching as she caved into herself. The stress of everything was beginning to get to her. But she couldn't let that happen.

A strong hand covered her shoulder. She opened her eyes and saw Levi standing there, looking at her with those warm eyes that seemed to read into her soul in a way that should make her uncomfortable. But for some reason it didn't.

"I'm sorry, Rebecca. I know this is difficult."

As he said the words, a contraction hit, and Rebecca nearly doubled over.

"Rebecca? Is it the baby?"

She tried to straighten herself. She wanted to pretend that everything was okay. But she couldn't fake it, not if it put her baby at risk.

"I don't know." The pain subsided, but Rebecca's muscles were still poised for another round of discomfort.

"Maybe I should take you to the doctor." Levi grasped her arm.

She started again to say that she was fine. She was so used to the words rolling off her tongue. But instead, she nodded. "I think maybe that's a good idea."

Levi led her back to his car. He climbed in and wasted no time driving down the road to the clinic.

Thank goodness he'd been close. He was definitely a godsend.

But too much uncertainty still remained on the horizon.

CHAPTER NINE

LEVI TRIED NOT to pace the waiting room area. But all he could think about was Rebecca and her baby. Whoever was behind these acts may not have directly harmed her, but their actions were putting her at risk. It was all the more reason he needed to find answers.

Maybe he should tell her the truth.

His spine stiffened at the thought. No, telling her wasn't part of the plan. Coming here, Levi had agreed to go undercover in order to find answers. But it would be so much easier if he was just straightforward about his true intentions.

He wrestled with the thought. The compassionate side of him collided with the professional. He'd been sent here to do a job, and he needed to do it. And he could do these things at his own discretion, but—

At the thought, his cell phone rang. He looked at the screen and saw it was his boss, Ed Helmer. He sighed before putting the phone to his ear.

"Levi," Ed said. "How are things going so far?"

"I'm not making quite as much progress as I had hoped."

"That's not good enough. You know we don't have a lot of time. If we aren't careful, these guys will slip away. We can't let that happen."

Levi bit down before saying, "Yes, I know that. I'm working as hard as I can. Sometimes you can't force these things."

"What about the wife? Did you get any information from her?"

The wife? No, it was Rebecca, he silently corrected.

Levi paced toward the vending machines and away from anyone who might be listening. "Like I said, I'm working on it."

"And, like I said, you need to work harder. We need to figure out if she's involved."

Rebecca's face stained his thoughts. Her innocent eyes, her vulnerability, the protective way she rubbed her stomach. "I don't think she's involved with this."

"And why do you think that?" Ed's voice sounded hard, determined. All the man wanted was answers, for the bad guys to get their justice.

"It's what my gut tells me."

"We all know that guts have a tendency to be wrong. I need proof."

Levi's stomach twisted. If it were any other job, he might recommend sending somebody else in right now. But somebody else might not be as compassionate toward Rebecca as he was. Levi couldn't stand that thought. Even though he hadn't known the woman long, she brought out a protective side of him.

"None of this is because of Brianna, is it?"

At the sound of her name, Levi tensed again. He glanced over his shoulder again, making sure no one was near. "This has nothing to do with Brianna. That was five years ago. It's in the past."

"But I know that it shook you. I had some reservations about sending you, considering your past."

"I can handle this." Levi's jaw tightened.

"Good. Prove me wrong. Prove that you can handle this. I'm counting on you."

Levi put his phone away. He felt even less settled

now than he did earlier. How was he going to find the answers he needed while keeping a clear conscience?

He had no idea. But he would figure out a way. He had no other choice.

REBECCA STEPPED out of the exam room a few minutes later, Doc Clemson by her side. She wasn't sure if Levi would wait around for her or if she would need to call a ride to get back to her house.

She secretly hoped that Levi would still be there, which was ridiculous. She hardly knew the man, and just because he'd rode into her life like a knight in shining armor didn't mean he was someone she could—or *should*—depend on. She'd be wise to keep that in mind.

However, Rebecca would be lying if she didn't admit that her heart raced when she saw Levi standing in the distance. His hands were shoved down into the deep pockets of his black sweatshirt. His gaze looked heavy, concerned. Yet his stance was still upright, as if he were on guard.

As soon as Levi spotted her, he strode toward her.

His voice sounded tender as he paused a few steps away. "Is everything okay? How's the baby?"

Rebecca rubbed her belly. "Emma is doing fine. Thank you for bringing me by, just so I could have that peace of mind. It was just a Braxton Hicks contraction."

"But she does need to be careful." Doc Clemson stepped forward. "The stress and strain she's been under the past few weeks could send her into early labor. She's getting close enough to her due date that the baby will probably be fine, but we want to keep the baby in there as long as possible. She'll need someone to keep an eye on her."

Rebecca felt her cheeks heat at the thought. He seemed to think she and Levi were more than neighbors who'd just met.

"Don't worry him over these things," Rebecca said. "I'm going to do everything within my power to make my life as stress-free as possible."

Doc Clemson glanced at Levi and sent him a look.

The next thing she knew, Levi took her arm. "I'll make sure I keep an eye on her."

Part of Rebecca wanted to say that Levi didn't need to make a fuss over her. But it was more than her life on the line here.

She swallowed back her words and instead said, "Thank you."

Levi's warm gaze seemed to see into her soul as he observed her a moment. "How about if I give you a ride back home?"

She nodded a little too quickly. "I suppose the chief is waiting there."

"I believe she's wrapping things up now," Levi said. "But she wanted to wait to ask you a few questions. I can tell her if you don't feel up to it—"

"No, of course I can talk to her. It's no problem. Plus, I need to check to see if anything was taken."

"Do you think it's a good idea if you stay at your place tonight?" Doc Clemson asked.

Where else would she stay? Rebecca supposed she could stay with her best friend, Layla. But Layla and her husband were out of town right now. Layla had purposely chosen to go on vacation this week so she could be here when Rebecca had her baby.

There were other people she could stay with, but Rebecca hated to put anyone out. She was going to have to think this through. Plus, at heart, she was a homebody. She found a lot of comfort being in her own space, around her own things.

"I promise I'll be careful and that I'll figure

things out," Rebecca said. "And I will take all of the precautions that you told me to take. I promise."

Doc Clemson squeezed her elbow. "If you need me, you know I'm just a phone call away."

"Yes, I know. Thank you."

She turned to Levi and felt a rush of relief go through her again. Life was so much easier when you had people to depend on, to help with the heavy lifting. "If you wouldn't mind driving me home ..."

"Of course. Let me know whatever you need, and I'll be happy to help."

But his words were bittersweet. Soon he'd be leaving, she reminded herself. She couldn't afford to let herself get too close.

CHAPTER TEN

LEVI ARRIVED with Rebecca back at her place. The police chief was still there with one of her officers, wrapping things up as Levi and Rebecca stepped into the house.

Chief Chambers rushed toward them, briefly giving Levi another warning glance before she turned to address Rebecca. "Everything good?"

Rebecca rubbed her stomach. "Emma is doing just fine."

Chambers offered a quick smile and led Rebecca to one of the dining room chairs. "I'm glad the doctor said that everything is okay. I'm sure he also told you that you need to take care of yourself."

"I never realized what a big job that was."

Rebecca frowned as she leaned back in the stiff wooden chair.

Chambers lowered herself into a seat across from Rebecca and squeezed her arm. "I realize this isn't a good time, but I need to know if anything was taken."

Rebecca's gaze scanned her house, and she shrugged. "I don't really have anything of value. My gut tells me someone did this as more of a means to send a message than anything else. Am I right?"

Chambers frowned, her gaze focused on Rebecca. "I can't tell you that. It's strange that this has happened two days in a row. It definitely has me concerned. I'm going to station an officer outside your house this evening, just to keep an eye on things."

Rebecca's eyes widened, as if the implications of the past two days were finally settling in her mind. "Thank you. I appreciate that. Maybe I'll sleep better knowing I have somebody watching my back."

"You have a lot of people watching your back," Chambers said. "If you would like to, you're more than welcome to come and stay with Ty and me. You know we have plenty of space."

"If worse comes to worst, I will. But what I want more than anything right now is just to stay home and get my house in order. It's just a matter of time before baby Emma comes. I don't feel like I've done nearly enough."

"I saw the nursery upstairs," Chambers said. "It looks beautiful. The important thing is I know this little girl will be loved."

Rebecca rubbed her stomach again and seemed to suck back her emotions. "Yes, she will be."

Levi saw the moisture that welled in Rebecca's eyes. This was taking a toll on her. It would be stressful enough for the average person, but with a pregnancy added to the mix, it had to be overwhelming. He reminded himself that he needed to remain on guard, though. The woman was quickly making a way into his heart, and he couldn't let that happen.

"If I notice anything that's been taken as I clean up this mess, I'll let you know." Rebecca rolled her shoulders back, her gaze becoming more focused.

"I heard back about Jared also." The chief's lips curled down in a frown. "He was on Hatteras. It wasn't him who followed you."

The air left Rebecca's lungs. If not Jared, then who?

"We're still looking for the black car. I have a feeling the driver dumped it somewhere. We'll find it eventually."

Rebecca nodded. "Thank you for the update."

Chambers leaned closer, and her voice turned less professional. "I get off work in a couple hours. I can come by and help you out here."

"Let me see what I can get done on my own." Rebecca's gaze scanned the devastation around her. "But I appreciate the offer. And I'll call you if I need help."

The police chief nodded again. "Do you promise?"

"Yes, I promise," Rebecca said.

As soon as the chief left, Levi turned to Rebecca. "Let me help you clean things up."

Her head drooped to the side in either exhaustion or bewilderment. She rested her cheek against her hand.

Her voice sounded tired as she said, "You've already done so much. I couldn't possibly ask you to do that."

"But I don't mind."

She raised her head long enough for her gaze to search his. "What about your work?"

Levi shrugged. "I can officially say that I'm not getting any work done today. Besides, I'm not going to be able to sit over at my house relaxing while I think about you over here cleaning up this mess by yourself. Let me help."

Rebecca pressed her lips together for a moment, and Levi was uncertain what she would say. But he couldn't press any more than he already had. It would only raise warning flags.

"If you don't mind, then I would appreciate having an extra hand. My back is sore, and I'm not sure I can do this all on my own. But I know I won't get any rest until it's straightened."

"I'd be more than happy to help." Not only did he truly want to offer a hand, but this would also be the perfect excuse to look for answers.

Guilt bit at him at the thought. But he'd come here to do a job. He never would have guessed that his target would be so lovely or that he'd find this assignment so difficult.

And he was going to have to figure out what to do about that.

REBECCA FELT as if she'd known Levi for months instead of mere days. How was it possible since they'd just met?

As they worked, he told stories to try to distract

her. Despite that, Rebecca's thoughts kept going back to everything that had happened. When she let her guard down, worry filled her.

She tried to keep the emotion at bay, but it was becoming harder and harder. She was exhausted. Knowing that an elevated stress level made her pregnancy more difficult unfortunately caused her stress to hike even higher. It seemed like a vicious cycle.

Rebecca tried to swallow down the emotions. But the combination of everything that had happened made it hard.

As she sat by her entertainment center and placed photo albums back on the shelves, Rebecca's gaze caught a picture of her with her late husband. Tears rushed to her eyes again.

The two had met when Jim moved to Lantern Beach, only intending on staying here for the summer and waiting tables at a local restaurant. They met when Jim scheduled a charter fishing trip and Rebecca had gone along to help her cousin, who was the captain.

It had felt like love at first sight. Jim had ended up moving here permanently and finding a job with the management company.

Three years in, things started to go downhill.

The memories battered her.

Emma should have a dad. She should have all the right ingredients to have a happy childhood.

Instead, Rebecca's daughter would have a single mom struggling to make ends meet. Sometimes it didn't feel fair that Rebecca was bringing a child into the world under those circumstances.

She knew that probably wasn't rational, yet all she could think about were the qualities that she lacked. How would she make up for those things? How would Emma be affected by them?

The baby hadn't even been born yet, but all Rebecca wanted was the best for her child. Instead, she had tons of unanswered questions and less-than-fond memories about Emma's father.

She stared at the picture again. It showed one of their happier moments together. They'd gone to the beach for a bonfire, and they'd had a good heart-to-heart talk about their future.

This photo showed the early days of marriage. Before the two of them had realized that they probably wouldn't be able to have kids. Before accusations had been thrown out against him, causing Jim to lose his job and for his reputation to be ruined.

Sure, they'd had their struggles back then. Like every newly married couple, they'd had issues they had to work through. But when this photo had been taken, Rebecca had no idea about what was to come.

She felt another round of tears rush to her eyes. She stood, realizing she couldn't look at these pictures anymore.

She paced into the kitchen, where Levi placed scattered silverware into the dishwasher. "I just wanted to let you know, that I'm going to step outside onto the deck for a minute."

Levi looked up, holding a handful of spoons. "Take all the time you need."

She was thankful for his understanding. Because the events of the past few days would be enough to scare off most reasonable people.

CHAPTER ELEVEN

AS SOON AS Rebecca disappeared from sight, Levi's muscles tightened. He remembered his conversation with Ed, and he glanced around Rebecca's house. The one place where there would most likely be evidence was Rebecca's desk. It was located in the corner of the dining room.

Levi stepped from the kitchen and paced down the hall. Rebecca stood on the deck, leaning against the railing and staring out into the distance. The sight clutched his heart, but he tried to push those emotions away. She was going through a lot and just needed some time to herself.

Levi hesitated a moment, torn between going to her and doing his job.

This was his best chance to find information. He

90

swallowed his guilt, hoping he didn't hate himself for what he had to do.

Moving quickly, Levi went to the desk and pulled out a drawer. He riffled through everything. There were bills and pictures and paperclips. Nothing of interest.

He moved on to the next drawer. More of the same—envelopes, stamps, sticky notes.

He opened the last drawer.

Business cards were scattered there. His fingers splayed through them, looking for anything of note. Most were nothing.

But he stopped at one.

Wilford Black.

His throat tightened.

Wilford was one of the men he was investigating. This business card listed his title as a mortgage appraiser. But Levi knew the man was much more than that.

The question was: Did this card belong to Rebecca? Or had it been her husband's?

Levi thought he knew the answer, but he had to be careful. He'd already been betrayed once. He'd never be able to show his face around his colleagues if he let it happen again.

As he peered down the hallway at the deck, he

saw Rebecca was still standing there leaning against the railing. Except this time her shoulders shook.

His heart lurched. He knew what that meant.

She was crying.

After only a moment of hesitation, he shoved the card into his pocket and started her way. Softly, he opened the back door and stepped out onto the deck.

He didn't want to surprise her. Instead he called, "Hey."

Rebecca didn't even look over her shoulder. Instead she offered a subtle rise of her shoulders to let him know she'd heard him.

Levi paced toward her and leaned against the deck beside her. He'd been right. Moisture streamed down her face. She quickly wiped her cheeks with the back of her hand and then pulled her sweater closer.

"Can I get you a blanket or anything?" Levi's voice cut into the silence. "It's cold out here."

"I'm okay. Thank you."

He wondered for a moment what he could say or do that could possibly make her feel better. He knew the truth: very little could make her feel better.

Instead, he just stood there with her, waiting to see if she would say something on her own.

When she finally spoke, her voice sound hoarse. "I feel so ill-equipped."

"What do you mean?" His heart thrummed in his throat.

Rebecca stared off into the darkness beyond the house. "I mean, I'm about to bring a baby into this world. I should have more things figured out than I do."

"You have the most important things figured out," Levi said. "For example, you know that you already love this baby inside you."

Rebecca rubbed her belly again, that soft look coming to her eyes. "I do love Emma, even though I haven't seen her face-to-face yet."

"What else do you need to know?"

She drew in a long, shaky breath. "Practical things. Like I need to know how I'm going to show houses and act as a realtor when I have a baby with me. I need to know how I'm going to pay my bills when the clients don't roll into town or when a big hurricane comes and shuts everything down for a month. I need to know I'll be able to feed my child when she's hungry."

The raw authenticity of her words caused Levi's heart to throb in his ears. "Has money been that tight?"

"There are times when it is. Like I said, it's just going to be hard to work and take care of a newborn. I never anticipated doing this alone."

He placed his hand on her back. "It seems like you have a great community surrounding you. I know people will step in to help out."

"I know they want to. I don't know why I'm worrying so much. I'm usually not such an overreactor. I promise."

"You're pregnant. It's going to heighten your emotions."

She let out a soft laugh and shook her head. "Yes, you are probably right. I told you I'm kind of a mess right now."

"If this is you in a mess, then you must be even more fantastic on a normal day."

Rebecca cast a quick smile. But it faded all too soon. She drew in a deep breath, and Levi braced himself for what she was going to say next.

"I know this might sound crazy, Levi." Her wide eyes met his. "I can't help but think that maybe my baby is the target here."

He sucked in a deep breath at her words. "What do you mean?"

Her hands protectively went over her belly. "I mean, what if whoever has been targeting me over the past two days isn't really targeting me? The only thing I have of value is my baby."

As the words washed over him, Levi sucked in another breath. What if she was right?

REBECCA WIPED AWAY HER TEARS, feeling foolish at the words that had just left her mouth. What was Levi going to think of her? She knew her theory sounded absurd, but she couldn't stop thinking about it. How was she going to keep her baby safe?

"I'm right next door." Levi's voice sounded kind and concerned, not at all judgmental as she had feared. "If there's anything you need, anything at all, I can be here in thirty seconds flat. We are not going to let anything happen to your baby."

She didn't know if it made her feel better or worse to know that he thought her idea might have some validity. Despite her indecision, she rolled her shoulders back and raised her chin.

"Why would somebody want my baby?" Rebecca's throat burned as soon as the words left her lips. They sounded so awful to say aloud.

Levi stepped closer. The stillness of the night

seemed to pause even further around them. Gone was the earlier rain and sharp wind. For the moment, everything felt crisp and peaceful.

Even the scent of the ocean seemed a spa-like aroma at the moment, beckoning relaxation and deceleration. "For starters, we don't know that for sure. Yes, there are some psychos in the world who like to target pregnant women. But that doesn't mean that's the case with you right now."

Rebecca turned toward him, her gaze probing Levi's "Then what else could it be? Why else would all of this be happening?"

"That's a good question. I'm sure the police chief is working to figure that out now."

"I mean, there have been break-ins. That mysterious car. My bank account. What's going on?"

Levi shifted, turning to face her more. "You have no idea why somebody might do any of those things? There have been no other hints of trouble before yesterday?"

She shook her head. "No, not that I know of. I mean, I pretty much keep to myself. I sell houses, and I go to church."

"Have there been any real estate deals lately that have been contested? Did you maybe sell a fore-closed home or something similar?"

"I did assist in selling one of those a month or two ago. But it wasn't contested. The owner walked away from the house and moved back to Georgia. I have a hard time thinking that has anything to do with this."

Levi shifted, his gaze appearing far-off in thought. "What about your husband? I hate to ask it, but could any of this be tied to him?"

Jim? Could this really have something to do with her former husband? "I don't know how. I mean, sure, he had his issues. But did he have issues that would put me in danger? I have trouble seeing it."

"What did he do when he left you? Where did he go? How did he earn money?"

Rebecca let out a long breath. "I don't really know. He left, and we lost contact. He wouldn't return my calls. I had no idea where he went."

"And after he died?"

"I know it's going to sound strange and sad, but after I heard that he was dead, I just started to plan his funeral. I didn't look into what he had been doing. I figured he probably found an old friend from college and crashed on his couch. Jim didn't seem extremely motivated to bring in any money."

"Then how was he paying for this life insurance policy that he took out for you?"

It was a good question. Rebecca had thought of that herself but had pushed aside her concerns, chiding herself for overthinking things. The thought reminded her that she was supposed to get back with Patrick.

That wouldn't be happening today. She could hardly think straight.

It could wait until tomorrow—especially in light of Levi's question. She needed more time to think, to process.

"To be honest, I'm not sure how he paid for the policy," Rebecca finally said. "I assumed he took a job to earn a few bucks."

Levi's gaze locked on hers. "So there's no chance he got himself caught up in trouble?"

"I really can't see it." Rebecca let out another breath, the weight of this conversation leaving her feeling spent. "Thank you for listening. I guess we should continue to clean up. Or, honestly, I'm pretty exhausted. I think I will call it a night and pick up in the morning."

Levi nodded, but a new emotion entered his gaze. Was that disappointment?

"Remember, I'm next door." Levi handed her a business card with his company name and cell phone listed. "Just call me if you need me."

Comfort wrapped around her like a warm blanket at the thought. "Thank you."

But the feeling quickly faded, replaced with a stark coldness.

She was in this alone, and she'd be wise to remember that.

CHAPTER TWELVE

REBECCA WOKE the next morning to a pounding at her door. She quickly threw some clothes on and rushed downstairs.

When she opened the door, she saw Officer Bradshaw standing there with a man she'd never seen before. He wore a suit, which was the first sign that something was up. Most people on Lantern Beach didn't wear suits.

Tension crawled over her muscles. "Good morning. Can I help you?"

"Hi, Ms. Jarvis," Officer Bradshaw said. The cop was in his mid-twenties with dark hair and a strong jaw. He was one of the newer additions to the police department. "This man just arrived and wants a few minutes of your time. I wanted to run that past you first."

Rebecca turned back to the strange man. Before she could ask any questions, he extended his arm and handed her a card. As he spoke, her gaze scanned the words there. "I'm Special Agent Stephenson with the FBI, and I'd like to ask you a few questions."

"Concerning what?" She had no idea why the FBI would show up right now.

The agent frowned at Officer Bradshaw, acting as if he didn't want the man to be privy to the conversation. "I can tell you out here, but I would prefer some privacy. When you hear what I have to say, I think you'll want that privacy also. But it's your choice."

Rebecca's gaze skimmed Officer Bradshaw again, and she nodded. "I'll go inside for a minute. If you'd stay here on the porch, I'd appreciate it."

The officer nodded. "Yes, ma'am. I'll be right here if you need me."

If this man was an FBI agent, Rebecca didn't see why she would need the police officer. But she still felt cautious and leery of strangers right now. Having Bradshaw close provided an extra safety measure.

She led Agent Stevenson into her house and

offered him a seat at the kitchen table. "I don't have any coffee ready yet, but I can make some if you would like."

"I'll be fine. But thank you." The agent shifted in his seat. The man was tall and lean with faded blond hair and a vanishing hairline. His eyes were icy blue and his motions strictly professional—almost unnervingly so. "Ma'am, I have a few questions for you. I'm sorry to show up unannounced like this."

Rebecca pulled her hair back into a quick ponytail, wishing she'd had time to clean up a bit. Not only that, but she wished she'd had time to collect her thoughts. "I have to admit that I'm a little more than curious about why you're here."

"I've been investigating some weapons that have been smuggled into the country. As I have been researching these guys, I discovered a link to you."

Her eyes widened. "A link to me?"

"Or, maybe I should say, a link to your late husband."

The wind left her lungs, and she leaned back hard in her chair. At once, she remembered what Doc Clemson had told her about her stress levels. She couldn't afford to get worked up about this. Not yet, at least.

"I have no idea what you're talking about. But I would love for you to explain."

Stephenson tapped his finger against the table before responding. "There is a chain of weapons smugglers who have been operating along the East Coast. They're using unoccupied buildings to hide these weapons until they get to their destinations. Your husband's name came up during the course of the investigation, and I need to know everything you know about it."

She felt another cramp in her stomach coming on. She closed her eyes and began praying that her baby would be okay. This wasn't what she needed right now.

"My husband and I were separated before he died. He left and didn't look back. I have no idea what went on during those months of his life. If he got into trouble, he didn't tell me about it."

"So, you know nothing about any deals that he was making?"

"No, why would I?" Rebecca stood, suddenly feeling like she needed some of that coffee. She went to the pot and began spooning grounds into the filter.

"Because my investigation has led me to believe

that one of the houses you're representing was used for these weapons that have been smuggled."

Rebecca grabbed the counter so she could keep her balance. Otherwise, she might double over. Instead, she grabbed a pitcher and filled it with some water, desperate to do something before the FBI agent thought she was guilty.

"One of my houses?" she asked. "There's no way I would ever let that happen."

Stephenson remained unfazed, his gaze intense as he watched her every move. "Did you ever have a house that went untouched for more than a month at a time?"

Carefully, she poured the water into the pot and hit the On button before turning back to him. That coffee couldn't brew fast enough.

"On occasion, I'll take on a property like that," she started. "However, I usually have little hope of selling it because of the condition that it's in. At times, I won't even schedule any showings, cleanings, or staging. But those rare cases would be the only times that I will leave one of my properties untouched for that amount of time."

"Are you familiar with the property at 23148 Coastal Shores Drive?"

She instantly pictured the old fishing cabin. "That's the old house near the Pamlico Sound."

"I take that as a yes."

"No one's lived there for years, but, when the parents passed away, the son wanted to put it on the market. He didn't want to do any improvements in the meantime, however. Is that what this is about? Because I haven't been in that house in more than a month. In fact, I was going to suggest to the son that he let another realtor represent it."

Agent Stephenson continued to coolly observe her, his pale blue eyes continuing to watch her every expression and move. "We believe that is where some of the criminal activities have been operating out of."

"Why in the world would you think my late husband was involved?" Rebecca resisted the urge to shake her head. What the agent had told her didn't make sense.

He reached into his pocket and pulled out a picture of Jim standing with three other men. The photo had been taken in the dark, making it hard to make out details. But something about the other men—about their body language, the way they dressed, their tattoos even, made Rebecca realize these men weren't talking about sports.

"Who are they?" The words burned as they left her lips.

"Members of the Spades."

"Who are the Spades?"

"They're a weapons-smuggling ring—gunrunners, if you will. They mostly operate out of the East Coast, and they're deadly. Ruthless. Not people you want to mess with."

She swallowed so hard she nearly choked.

Stephenson continued. "This guy right here is the ringleader." He pointed at the man who wore all black. "The leader's name is Wilford Black. Does he look familiar?"

Was he the man who'd broken into her home? Rebecca had no idea. "I can't say he does."

Despite that, all the blood drained from her face. What had Jim gotten himself involved in? Was that the source of her trouble now?

He hadn't made things right. He'd made them ten times worse.

LEVI WATCHED from his window as a police officer led the suited man to Rebecca's front door. His curiosity piqued.

He wished he had a closer relationship with Rebecca, that he had known her longer. Because more than anything he wanted to march over there and make sure everything was okay. But he would be crossing some kind of invisible boundary if he did so.

Instead, he remained at the window watching and waiting. Based on the way the man was dressed, he was some kind of official. But Levi had no idea who.

Was it the life insurance salesman? Was all of this about the insurance payout? Or was this about her baby? He could barely stomach the thought of it.

He skipped his coffee and checked his messages while keeping an eye on the house. Finally, after an hour, the man left. Now Levi needed to figure out a way to subtly ask her some questions without raising her suspicions. But he wasn't quite sure how to do that.

To his surprise, he saw her walk from her house and cross the lawn between their places. The next instant, Rebecca knocked on his door.

Levi breathed a sigh of relief. That had been easier than he had thought. He had to admit that Rebecca touched something inside him that he hadn't felt in a long time. He still planned on investigating this case, but his perspective had been changed since he arrived in town and met Rebecca.

Stay on guard, he reminded himself. *Don't make the same mistake twice.*

He drew in a deep breath. Was Rebecca a wolf in sheep's clothing? He didn't want to believe it. But he did need to be careful.

He opened the door and quickly observed Rebecca's demeanor. She looked ashen and her hands trembled. Not a good sign.

Levi stepped toward her and took her arm. "Rebecca?"

She shook her head. "I'm sorry to come over here so early, I just didn't know who else to talk to."

"Come on in." He led her to the couch and waited until she was seated to release her arm. "Can I get you something to drink?"

She shook her head. "No, I'm fine. Well, I'm not fine, but I don't need any coffee. I'm already wired enough."

"What's going on?" He lowered himself a comfortable distance away on the couch, though his desire was to sit close in case she needed him.

"I don't know why I'm coming over here to tell you this. Maybe it's because you'll leave this island one day and if this turns out to be a disaster, I'll never have to see you again."

For some reason, the thought of never seeing her again did something strange to his heart. Would he be able to walk away from this assignment one day, acting as if he'd never met her? He wasn't sure. That would be a question for another day.

"I've been told I'm a pretty good listener. So what's going on? You look shaken." As Levi said the words, he glanced at her arms. They trembled uncontrollably. And her breaths came quickly. Probably too quickly.

She ran a hand over the top of her blonde hair, leaving her ponytail lopsided. "I know how this is going to sound. The people here on the island might even think less of me if they find out. But I don't know what else to do."

"Rebecca, what's going on?" He tried to put the pieces together, but he had no idea.

"A man stopped by my house this morning. He's with the FBI."

His eyes widened. He should have known. But why were they involved in this? This wasn't their territory. "Why would the FBI stop by your house?"

"That's what I asked when the agent first arrived. He went on to tell me that he believes my late husband was involved in a weapons-smuggling operation. Isn't that the craziest thing you have ever heard?"

"A weapons-smuggling operation? That sounds like something straight from Hollywood." Levi kept the surprise in his voice, even though he knew it was the truth.

It killed him to say that, to act like this. He could answer so many questions for her. Yet if he did that, Rebecca would know the truth about who he was and why he was here. He might not ever find out any answers then and know if she was truly innocent or guilty—although he thought he already knew the truth.

Rebecca went on to tell him about how one of the properties that she represented was believed to have been used for storing smuggled weapons. Levi had also heard that.

"So they think that you're involved in this?" Levi leaned closer, anxious to hear what else she had to say.

Rebecca buried her face, her breath escaping in a rush of emotion. "Apparently, they do. They've been keeping their eye on me for a while. I just don't understand. I would never do something like that. I know money has been tight, so that means I've just been working harder. It doesn't mean I've turned to anything illegal."

He licked his lips and chose his words carefully. "What about your late husband? Could you see him getting mixed up in something like that?"

Rebecca hesitated, which was an answer within itself. "I don't want to think that Jim would ever do something like that. But the truth is, in the past year or so, I didn't even feel like I knew him. And what *did* he do when he left here? What if this is all true?"

He leaned forward and squeezed her hand. "Rebecca, even if it is true, you're going to get through this."

"Not if they think I'm involved! If they think that I had any part in this, I'm going to jail. Who's going to take care of my baby?" She wiped more moisture from her face.

"Did you tell them about the threats against you? That should prove you're a victim instead of a perpetrator."

"I told him. I'm not sure what he thought about it. He was hard to read."

Levi hesitated a moment before saying, "Maybe I can help somehow."

She stared at him, doubt in her gaze. "I appreciate that offer, but I'm not really sure what an engineer is going to be able to do to help out in this situation."

She had a good point. Then again, she didn't know the whole truth either. "I know I'm just an engineer. But I'm pretty good at doing my homework. I've always been told I have an eye for detail. Maybe I can help do something."

"I would love it if you could. But I don't want to put you in the middle of a bad situation. I know I need to tell Cassidy—or Chief Chambers to you. But I'm just so afraid word of this is going to leak on the island."

"Do you think the chief is going to tell people?"

"It's not that I think she'll tell people. But if she starts investigating, people are going to start to talk. If my reputation is ruined, then my career will be done. I can't risk that."

Levi's jaw twitched. Rebecca told the truth. He couldn't deny that. In her line of work, reputation was everything. "Let me see what I can do for you. Do you have this FBI agent's name or number?"

She reached into her pocket and pulled out a card. "This is what he gave me."

Levi stared at the business card a moment before nodding. "Okay, this would be a great place to start. In the meantime, why don't you put your feet up and relax for a little while? Let me do some of the heavy lifting for a few minutes."

After a moment of hesitation, Rebecca nodded.

Levi stood. Maybe he'd finally figure out some answers.

CHAPTER THIRTEEN

LETTING somebody else take care of her was hard for Rebecca. Even though it was what she secretly craved sometimes, she'd been on her own for long enough now that she'd learned to do things for herself. The fact that Levi was bringing her drinks and food and insisting that she lie down felt foreign to her.

Cassidy had already stopped by and taken her statement. The chief was also going to look into what was going on. She'd promised discretion, and Rebecca trusted her enough to believe that she would act on her promise.

Meanwhile, Levi had been on Rebecca's computer, and he appeared to be looking some things up. She'd given him permission to look at whatever he needed as he tried to find answers.

Rebecca thought it was very sweet that he believed he could help. But she didn't know who could help her out in this situation. Sometimes, it felt too big for even local law enforcement. For goodness sake, the FBI had come to her house!

She thought she'd had trouble before, but now the pressure on her felt tripled. She must be desperate if she was relying on the stranger next door to help her out. But Rebecca didn't know who else she could turn to.

Levi appeared back in the living room, a grim look on his face as he held her laptop.

"What? What is it?" She pushed herself up, trying to look entirely more composed than she felt.

He pointed to the screen. "I searched your computer, including the junk mail, and I found an email from a bank."

"Okay? Most of them are scams. They want you to click and give your information, just so they can steal your money."

He sat down beside her and showed her the email. "I think this one is legit. It says there's a new bank account set up for you."

She sucked in a breath as his words settled on

her. "What? That's ridiculous. I didn't set up a new bank account."

Levi gave her a look, a mix of compassion and concern. "I believe you didn't. But what if someone else did?"

It took Rebecca a moment to understand what he was implying. "You think Jim did?"

"I think it's a possibility."

She didn't even know what to think. Wouldn't he have told her that? Wouldn't the bank have informed her? Did they even do that via email? Rebecca probably wouldn't have believed the news if the bank had called her.

She tried to formulate a response, but she had nothing. Jim had set up that life insurance policy without telling her ...

Maybe everything boiled down to this money.

Money that he could have potentially stolen from Ron.

She didn't want to believe it was true, but she had to consider that possibility.

Her phone buzzed, reminding her of an upcoming appointment. She put her feet on the floor and stood, weariness pressing down on her again. "Thanks for sharing. I'll have to do more research later. Unfortunately, I've got a showing that I need to do now."

"Are you sure that's a good idea?" Concern ricocheted through Levi's voice, and he narrowed his eyes.

Rebecca smoothed the wrinkles from her black slacks and straightened her sweater. "I can't afford to miss out on any deals."

"Do you need me to go with you?" Levi stood also and started to reach for her but dropped his hand.

The idea was sweet, but how professional would it look if Rebecca had a friend along with her as she showed houses today? As long as she paid attention to things around her, she should be okay.

"No, I'll be fine," she said. "I met this guy last week. He is an investor who already has eight other properties under his belt across the country. I think I should be fine."

"I don't mind . . ."

It was awful sweet of Levi, but she'd already imposed enough. "Thanks again, but I'll be careful."

"If you have a chance, check in later. Please."

She smiled. "Thanks. I will."

LEVI CHOMPED DOWN SO HARD that his jaw began to ache. He didn't think it was a good idea for Rebecca to go anywhere by herself right now. He wished he could have thought of a way to convince her not to, but his hands were tied.

At least, she knew the truth about her husband now. Certainly, it hadn't been easy to hear the facts, but it was important that Rebecca have a better idea of what she might be up against. Because that was what this was all about, wasn't it?

Her late husband had gotten himself involved in some dirty business. That's where he had made his money and also where he had found his trouble— trouble he'd passed on to Rebecca.

Levi needed to figure out his next play. He'd poked around on Rebecca's computer, but he hadn't found any evidence there. Jim obviously hadn't used it for any of his "business."

Besides that, Levi couldn't pretend to have discovered too many facts. That in itself would be suspicious. Rebecca already seemed skeptical that an engineer could help her get to the bottom of this. She was right to be doubtful. That combination would have been weird.

He wanted to visit that home on Coastal Shores to see if the FBI had found anything there. But if he showed up, it would look too suspicious. Besides, certainly the FBI had checked out the house before talking to Rebecca. They'd already collected any evidence there.

That was the first Levi had heard about that particular house. How had the FBI found out before he did? Didn't they know that this was Homeland Security's case, not the FBI's? He was going to need to talk to Ed about this.

But Levi just couldn't get his mind off Rebecca being out there alone. Even if she trusted this man whom she was showing houses to, that didn't mean she would be safe out there in public. What if the man who'd broken into her place found her again? Until Levi had a face to go with the name, he was dealing with an unseen enemy.

Making a final choice, he grabbed his keys. He waited until he saw Rebecca emerge from her house. She was dressed in some nice slacks, a blouse, and a winter coat. She headed to her SUV, now looking put together, like nothing had happened.

After she climbed into her SUV and backed out of the driveway, Levi climbed into his own car and began following a safe distance behind her. He didn't want her to know that he was tailing her. But he wanted to be close in case something happened.

She pulled up to an oceanfront house. The three-story property probably cost at least a half million. A car was already in the driveway. A Mercedes.

Levi slowed and pulled into a carport two houses down, where Rebecca would be less likely to see him. He climbed out just long enough to take a picture of the man's license plate.

He would run it and see exactly who they were dealing with. Most likely, it was no one, but Levi wanted to be safe. At least they hadn't ridden together. That was a good thing.

He waited outside his car, listening for any signs of trouble. Right now, Rebecca greeted the man with a big smile, her professional persona shining brightly. If Levi hadn't seen her looking so upset earlier, he would never believe the emotional turmoil that was going on inside her right now.

Maybe she was a better actress than Levi had thought. The theory didn't settle well with him, though. He wanted to believe she was as trustworthy as the girl next door.

He continued to watch. Did he recognize that man? He didn't think so. Then again, this gang of weapons smugglers was deep. There was no way he could memorize or recognize all the faces involved. But he didn't like this. These guys were trouble.

Just then, a car pulled up behind him. Levi looked over, and his eyes widened.

Chief Chambers stepped out, her gaze narrowed with accusation.

Levi's stomach tightened. Based on the look in her eyes, Chief Chambers was on to him. How was he going to explain this?

CHAPTER FOURTEEN

REBECCA UNLOCKED the door to the oceanside mansion and opened it wide. "Sorry it's so cold in here, but the heat is turned down to fifty-five during the off-season."

The man, Roger Jenkins, rubbed his hands together and smiled. "It's no problem. I completely understand."

Jenkins appeared to be a businessman. She would guess him to be in his early sixties, and he carried himself like someone with money. She couldn't pinpoint what that reason was exactly. But he walked with confidence and spoke concisely.

She waited for him to slip past. Rebecca could hardly wait to see his face when he saw the view from the deck. It never got old watching the awe and wonder on people's faces when they saw the ocean views.

His gaze scanned the interior of the place. "This is fantastic."

"I know. I think so too. Anyone would be fortunate to have this house, and it has a great rental history. Large families love to come here."

"I can see why."

"I'll be happy to show you the rental history. For now, why don't you take a look around, and I'll meet you back here when you're done?"

"That sounds good." He offered a curt nod.

As soon as he walked away, Rebecca released the breath she held and her shoulders relaxed. When she was showing houses, she felt like she needed to be "on." She had to put her best foot forward and become a salesman.

But, despite the façade she wore now, her thoughts kept going back to everything that had happened. She was usually very private, and it took a lot for her to share things with people. But it was like she had told Levi—knowing that she may not ever see him again in another month gave her just enough courage to open up. It also made her strangely sad.

As she waited for Mr. Jenkins to return, she

remained in the foyer and quickly checked her messages on her phone. There was nothing of interest, including no updates from the bank.

Her mind reviewed what she knew already, however.

The FBI was investigating her husband about a potential weapons-smuggling operation. Apparently, there was a lot of money involved. Did Jim make the wrong person mad? Was that person coming after her now? Rebecca shuddered at the thought.

First, there was the initial break-in. Then her money disappeared from her bank account, and she'd gotten that threatening text. Then someone chased her down the road, followed by a second break-in. What a nightmare.

She hoped she could make a sale. It would take a lot of pressure off her for the coming months. Selling a house like this would take care of her for the rest of the winter. It would be an answer to prayer.

Something on the floor caught her eye. A paper. It must have fallen out of Mr. Jenkins's pocket when he'd pulled his phone out earlier.

When she reached down to pick it up, her breath caught.

It was a picture. Her picture.

Fear tightened her muscles. Who was this man she was in the house with?

~

"DO you care to explain to me what you're doing here?" Chief Chambers had a fearless look in her eyes that proved she meant business. They remained in the stranger's driveway, both staring the other down.

Don't stare her down, Levi reminded himself. It would only seem suspicious.

Levi quickly considered his responses. "I was worried about Rebecca after everything that happened. So I thought I should come out here and keep an eye on her."

"Are you sure about that? Because it almost looks like you're stalking her." She twisted her head just enough to let him know she wasn't the gullible type.

Levi didn't need convincing.

"Stalking her?" Levi let out a gargled laugh. "I'm not stalking Rebecca. I can see where it might seem like that, but really, I'm just concerned."

"You know that none of this trouble started until you came to town."

He swallowed hard, realizing that the chief had a

point. "That might be true, but that doesn't mean I'm guilty."

"We like to look out for each other here in Lantern Beach. I'm sure I've mentioned that to you before." She crossed her arms as she waited for his response.

Levi made sure to soften his voice before saying, "Just because I'm a stranger doesn't mean I'm up to no good."

The chief crossed her arms and looked him up and down. "Why are you here in town, Levi?"

As a pause came in their conversation, the sound of waves crashing just beyond the dune filled the air. A slight drizzle had started, spattering across their skin.

Levi cleared his throat. "I told you, I was looking for a little getaway. Since I work remotely, I can go wherever I want."

"Yet you didn't go somewhere warm during the winter months?"

"Is that a crime?"

"No, it's not a crime. But I looked into your background."

Alarm raced through him. So she *was* investigating him. Unease grew in him.

"And what did you find out when you looked into my background?"

"That's the thing. I didn't find out anything. Your background is squeaky clean. You didn't even have a parking ticket."

"You say it like that's a bad thing."

"I'm just saying that there's something about you that doesn't ring true."

"I assure you that I have Rebecca's best interest at heart. I'm just trying to be a good neighbor."

Before the chief could say anything else, a scream ruptured the air. Levi and Chief Chambers look at each other before rushing toward the house.

Rebecca was in trouble.

CHAPTER FIFTEEN

REBECCA SCREAMED as Jenkins pulled a gun from beneath his jacket. She raised her hands in the air before quickly pulling them down over her belly. She had to protect Emma. Yet she felt so exposed, so helpless.

"Shut!" he demanded.

"What do you want?" Rebecca's voice quivered as the words left her lips.

"I think you know," Jenkins sneered, transforming from classy to malicious in the blink of an eye.

"I have no idea what you're talking about." Rebecca took a step back, desperate to put distance between herself and this man.

"You have something that belongs to me."

This was the man who'd sent her that text, wasn't it? He'd resorted to drastic measures. Yet he'd set this up last week, long before she'd received the text message.

Unless this wasn't the real Mr. Jenkins.

Despair deepened in her chest until an ache pounded inside her. "I have no idea what my late husband got mixed up in, but I assure you that I'm not involved."

His eyes narrowed as the smile on his vile lips grew wider. "But you are."

"What does that even mean?" Rebecca took another step back.

He leered before reaching for her. "You are coming with me."

Rebecca didn't know a lot about crime, but she knew enough to know that you never went with the bad guy. She would not come back alive if she did. Fear swept through her.

She jerked, pulling out of his grasp. But she knew this wasn't over.

"Can't we just talk this out?" Her voice cracked.

Emma. Emma was all she could think about.

"Time for talking is past," he growled. "Come with me."

Rebecca scooted back, wanting to get as far away

from the man as she could. But as she did, he raised his gun higher. "Don't make this difficult, Rebecca."

She glanced around looking for something to protect herself. But there was nothing. How was she going to get out of this situation? She should have let Levi come with her instead of being so stubborn.

Emma. All she could think about was Emma. She had to protect her baby no matter the cost. But how?

Jenkins reached for her again. This was it, she realized. The point of no return.

As despair pummeled her, the door behind her burst open. Rebecca gasped and turned. Cassidy and Levi charged inside.

Jenkins took off in a run toward the back of the house, and Cassidy took off after him.

He was gone, she realized. The man was gone, and Emma was okay.

Her knees buckled at the thought.

Levi caught her before she hit the ground and led her to the couch. She collapsed there, a trembling mess.

"Did he hurt you?" Levi asked, lowering himself beside her and reaching his arms out.

She fell into his embrace, feeling like she could no longer hold herself up. His strong arms pulled her closer, made her feel like no one could hurt her —for now, at least.

"I'm okay," she murmured. "You got here right on time. How did you know?"

"You'll have to forgive me, but I followed you here this morning. I was worried that something like this might happen."

She wanted to be mad, but how could she be? It was an invasion of her privacy, but it had saved her life. "And Cassidy?"

"She and I were on the same wavelength."

Levi pulled her closer, and Rebecca didn't argue. She had to focus on keeping herself calm instead. For Emma's sake.

Her gaze drifted to the back door where Cassidy had disappeared. She prayed that her friend was okay. Where was she? Had something happened?

"Maybe you should go check on her," Rebecca suggested.

"I don't want to leave you," Levi said. "Not until we know what's going on."

His words brought a rush of relief. Because Rebecca didn't want to be left alone either. Too much had happened. There was too much she was trying to comprehend right now.

A moment later, Cassidy strode back inside,

dragging Mr. Jenkins behind her. The man wore a scowl and his hands were cuffed behind him.

"Backup is on the way," Cassidy said. "I'm going to need to get a statement from you. I'd rather do it at the station. Does that work?"

"I can drive her," Levi said then turned to Rebecca. "I don't want to overstep, but I don't think you're in any condition to drive right now."

Rebecca knew better than to argue. He was telling the truth. She could barely walk in a straight line.

"Yes, I can go down there to give my statement."

As Cassidy led Jenkins away, he looked over his shoulder and gave Rebecca a look that chilled her to the bone. What was going on here? And how was she going to get out of it?

LEVI TOOK Rebecca to the station, where she gave her statement. She told Chief Chambers about how the man had pulled a gun on her and had demanded that she go with him. Thank goodness, he and the chief had arrived when they had. If Rebecca had gone with the man, Levi was certain they would never see her again.

He was hopeful that the police would get information from this man, the supposed Mr. Jenkins. Levi had no illusions that was the man's real name. Last he'd heard, the man had decided to shut up and wasn't saying a word. Not his real name, his age, nothing. The chief was going to have a long night ahead of her.

Rebecca had just been released to go home. So far, she seemed to be holding up okay physically. She hadn't had any more pains or any indications that there might be something wrong with her pregnancy. Levi knew Rebecca needed to get off her feet and rest. Now the challenge would be convincing her to let him help.

"Let's get you back home," he said.

She was obviously in a state of shock because she didn't even argue. Rebecca let him lead her out to his car. Hers was still at the other house. Later, they would figure out how to pick it up.

Rebecca said very little on the drive back. She stared out the window and rubbed her belly. The sight caused Levi's heart to twist again. He couldn't even imagine all she had been through.

At her house, Levi walked her to the door. Rebecca unlocked it and turned toward him. "Would you like to come inside for a minute?"

"I was hoping you would ask." He shrugged, trying not to look too eager.

A slight grin teased at her lips. He helped her inside. But when she went into the kitchen to try to act as hostess, he quickly shuttled her into the living room. "You need to sit down. Let me fix you something to eat and drink."

"I couldn't ask you to do that."

"You didn't ask me. I'm telling you that's what I'm going to do. You have had one tough day. One tough week, for that matter. And, honestly, I don't even want to take my eyes off you. Not until we know what's going on."

"We?" She stared at him.

Levi tried to lighten his own stance as he shrugged. "I know that's awfully pushy of me, and I'm sorry. I don't want to be that way, but with everything that's happened, I can't seem to help it."

"It's okay," she said. "I feel like I've known you for much longer than I actually have."

"I feel the same way."

The two of them shared a smile.

"Okay." Levi broke from his mood. "You sit down. I'm going to fix you something to eat. How does soup sound on this rainy day?"

"Soup sounds great. But I don't have anything canned."

"That's okay. I can whip up something from scratch." He had a few recipes up his sleeve.

"A man of many talents, I see."

He shrugged, not wanting to get her hopes up. "I don't know about that. I didn't say it would taste good."

She let out a laugh. Hearing that sound was music to his ears. It made his heart do a flip-flop. In fact, it might be the first real laugh he'd heard from her since they'd met. Levi would do anything to hear that sound again, to be in a different situation than the one that they were in now.

Had he lost his mind? How had his feelings for this woman developed so quickly? But he knew the truth. Circumstances like this could heighten emotions, could accelerate these kinds of things. He wasn't naïve enough to think otherwise.

But still, there was so much on the line. He had to figure out how to proceed. And he had to figure out if he was going to tell Rebecca the truth.

Rebecca had opened up to him. His job had been to get her to do so. But so much between them felt sincere, felt real.

CHAPTER SIXTEEN

WHATEVER LEVI WAS COOKING, it smelled wonderful. A savory aroma drifted from the kitchen, and Rebecca's stomach rumbled. A few minutes later, he appeared with a cup of warm water and placed it on the table near her.

"Here's something to hold you over until the soup is done. I want to give it another ten minutes or so to make sure the flavors blend. My mom always says you have to let the ingredients meld together."

Rebecca smiled as she took the warm water. "Your mom sounds like she was a pretty wise woman."

"There was no one quite like her."

Rebecca heard the grief in his voice. She recognized it from her own life. "Is your mom still alive?"

134

He rubbed his throat as the strands of "Blue Christmas" played in the background. "She is, but she was diagnosed with early onset Alzheimer's. She lives in a home up in Pennsylvania now. I try to stop in to visit her as often as I can."

"I can only imagine how difficult that is."

He shifted, throwing the dish towel over his shoulder and shrugging as he leaned against the doorway. "It is. Sometimes you feel like you're all alone in the world, you know?"

"Yeah, I totally understand that." The two exchanged a glance. "I lost my mom too. It doesn't feel right that I'm having a baby and she won't be here to give her advice."

"I'm sorry."

Rebecca took another drink of water. The warmth washed down into her system and instantly chased away her chills.

The man intrigued her, and she wanted to know more. "Tell me more about yourself. What do you do when you're not traveling for work?"

He let out a long breath and shrugged, as if the question required more thought than it should. "I like to mountain bike. At least, I used to."

"Why don't you anymore?"

He shrugged again. "No time, I guess. My dream

was always to go to Sedona and bike there. But life keeps getting in the way. Mainly, my job."

"Being an engineer must be demanding."

"You could say that."

She shifted on the couch and pulled a leg beneath her. "Then why don't you go to Sedona now? What's holding you back?"

"That's a great question."

As Rebecca set her drink down, she felt a thump in her stomach. Her hand went to her belly.

Levi sat beside her. His eyes were orbs of concern and kindness, and they made her heart melt just a little. How was it that she felt as if she'd known him weeks when it had only been days?

"Do I need to get the doctor?" Levi asked.

She waved a dismissive hand in the air. "Oh no. I'm fine. Sorry, it's just that Emma decided to kick me."

A smile spread across his face, and curiosity glimmered in his eyes. "Emma's moving around?"

Her hand moved over the spot, and she smiled. Feeling Emma move was one of the greatest joys in her life. "Yes, she's doing some kind of gymnastics right now."

"That's great."

She looked at Levi, a sudden and possibly crazy

idea entering her head. Before she could second-guess herself, she asked, "Would you like to feel?"

Levi's eyes lit, and he tilted his head. "Are you sure?"

"Absolutely."

Rebecca took his hand and placed it over the spot where Emma kicked. As soon as her belly moved again, a smile spread across Levi's face.

"That's the baby?" he asked, looking nearly spellbound with his wide eyes and lilted voice.

"Yes. Isn't that the coolest feeling? It still amazes me that I have a real human growing inside my body."

"That is absolutely amazing." He left his hand there another moment, and, when he removed it, Rebecca missed his touch. The thought was ridiculous. Why would she miss his touch? She hardly knew the man.

Rebecca knew she'd asked herself this a million times, but it still made no sense to her. Then again, the ways of the heart had never made much sense, did they?

As she and Levi looked at each other, their gazes locked. She felt herself being drawn to him, like an invisible thread pulled them closer. Did he feel it also? Could she even trust these feelings, or should she blame them on her pregnancy hormones?

Before either of them could say anything, do anything, the sound of the pot lid rattling in the distance drew their attention.

Levi stood, looking as frazzled as Rebecca felt as he ran a hand through his hair and let out a shaky breath. "I should go check that."

Rebecca nodded, probably too quickly. Maybe it was a good thing he had to leave to go into the kitchen. Because her heart was doing all kinds of flip-flops like she hadn't felt in a long time.

Her husband had left her seven months ago. Was that too soon to fall for somebody else? Certainly, it was too soon to fall for someone she just met a couple days ago. Rebecca wasn't calling this love. Not by any stretch of the imagination. But she definitely felt something was there.

If Rebecca was smart, she'd take a step back. She wouldn't let this go any further than a little infatuation.

Levi would be leaving soon. He wasn't here in Lantern Beach to stay, and it would be silly to think that they could somehow make things work long distance.

She was going to have a baby soon. Her plate

would be full. There would be no traveling out of town for a weekend visit up in Pennsylvania. Not with a newborn.

Rebecca should just put this all out of her mind.

She had a feeling that would be easier said than done.

REBECCA WOKE up the next morning with a start. She quickly pulled herself upright, confused for a moment as to where she was and what had happened.

Slowly, her living room came back into view. She had fallen asleep on the couch, she realized.

With Levi.

Her cheeks warmed. Somehow, she'd drifted to sleep with her head on his shoulder. The last thing Rebecca remembered was talking and laughing together. Levi had started a fire in the living room, she'd pulled a blanket over herself, and something about the coziness must have lulled her into slumber.

Her sudden movement must have awakened Levi. He blinked several times before raising his head from the back of the couch. His eyes still hazy,

Levi ran a hand over his face and turned to look at her. A lazy smile crept over his face.

"Good morning." His voice sounded deep and throaty with sleep.

"Good morning." Rebecca pushed her hair behind her ear, suddenly feeling self-conscious. "I . . . we must have . . ."

"I guess we were both exhausted from all the excitement yesterday. We must have both fallen asleep." He stood. "But I can go now. I never meant to impose—"

"You don't have to go yet." Her words surprised even her. "I mean, since you're here, why don't you stay for breakfast?"

He stared at her a moment, as if still uncertain. "Are you sure? I don't want to get your neighbors talking."

"You're my only neighbor still here at this time of year, so I think it will be okay. Besides, both you and I know the truth." As Rebecca said the words, her stomach tightened.

Braxton Hicks, she told herself. It wasn't a real contraction. She had been having these false alarms for the past few weeks. Since this was her first pregnancy, sometimes it was hard to tell what was real and what wasn't. She was starting to learn the difference.

Levi stepped closer, studying her with his gaze. "What's wrong?"

"It's nothing to be worried about. I promise. I would tell you if there was."

His shoulders relaxed ever so slightly, and he took a step away. "Why don't you relax and let me fix you something to eat?"

"If you keep spoiling me like this, I'm going to want to keep you around." Rebecca let out a brittle laugh, especially when she realized how Levi might take her words. Quickly, she rushed, "I'm joking."

He smiled, making it clear that he wasn't concerned. "It's not often that I get to cook for people, and I don't mind. Besides, I think that Clemson said you should try to stay off your feet as much as possible."

Rebecca didn't argue. Instead, she sat back down. "Thank you then."

"Let me go see what I can find in your kitchen."

Rebecca leaned back on the couch, somehow feeling incredibly peaceful in the middle of these dire circumstances. It was strange how the two opposing situations collided. The fact that someone seemed bent on tormenting her, combined with the fact that Levi had wandered into her life at just the right time.

He'd been a real lifesaver over the past few days, and she probably felt closer to him than she should.

That was a fact Rebecca was eventually going to have to deal with. But, for today, she would have breakfast. With Levi. And she would enjoy it.

CHAPTER SEVENTEEN

LEVI HAD to admit that he had been awake for a good portion of the night. He'd listened to everything around him. Looked for a sign that whoever was behind these recent activities had come back.

Plus, Rebecca had been sleeping so soundly on his shoulder. She'd softly breathed in and out, looking so at peace. Levi wished he could bottle the moment. He knew that peace wasn't something she'd been feeling a lot of lately.

He needed to tread carefully, though. Yes, he needed to get some answers. But he refused to let Rebecca be collateral damage.

Talking to her last night . . . it was the first time he'd felt real in a long time. It had felt good. It had made him miss having a normal life.

144

That was going to change, Levi vowed. One way or another, it would change.

He finished fixing an omelet with onions, peppers, and tomatoes. He'd also cut up some fruit and made some coffee. He placed it all on the table and called Rebecca to come eat.

She'd already gone upstairs to take a quick shower and change. When she joined him in the dining room, she was a sight to behold, with her wet hair, casual T-shirt, and yoga pants. The past few times he had seen her she had always been dressed professionally. Seeing her outfitted like this made her seem even more vulnerable. His heart clutched at the thought.

"This looks great." Rebecca gracefully waddled toward the table. "Thank you again so much for doing this."

He sat down across from her and picked up a fork. "Like I said, it's my pleasure."

A thought continued to weigh heavily on him. He knew so much about Rebecca, but there was so little he himself had shared. He couldn't share too much, but an internal urge nudged him to be real with her.

Levi opened his mouth. Then he shut it again. He couldn't tell her about his real job. Not yet. It could ruin the whole investigation. Yet he felt as if he could trust her.

He'd trusted Brianna also. He couldn't forget his past mistakes. He'd be foolish to do so.

"What is it?" Rebecca tilted her head, a soft glow about her. "You look like you have something on your mind."

Levi set his fork down and turned toward her. "I feel like we've grown close over the past few days, Rebecca."

She offered a shy smile. "I feel the same way. It's kind of strange, to be honest."

"I know what you're saying. Strange in a good way. At least, for me."

Her smile widened. "For me too."

"There's something I just feel like I need to tell you." He cleared his throat.

Rebecca's smile disappeared, replaced with doubt. Anxiety. Maybe even fear. "Of course. What's going on?"

He set his fork down, giving up on eating breakfast for the moment. "I was married."

Rebecca's eyes widened. "I wondered if you had ever been."

"Her name was Brianna. We were together three years."

"What happened?"

"She . . . cheated on me. Left me. Took me for everything she could get." That was the abridged version. She did cheat on him . . . but it wasn't how Rebecca probably assumed.

Rebecca reached across the table to grab his hand. "I had no idea. I'm so sorry, Levi."

He nodded, realizing how good it felt to get that off his chest—even if he hadn't shared all the details. "Me too. It was five years ago, but sometimes it feels like just yesterday."

"I can't imagine what that must have been like for you."

"It was difficult, to say the least."

The entire truth was that Brianna was working for one of the gangs Levi was investigating. The tables had been turned on him.

Brianna had cheated on him—but not with another man. She was working for the other side, and Levi had fallen for it hook, line, and sinker.

Rebecca squeezed his hand harder. "Thank you so much for sharing. It means a lot that you'd trust me enough to tell me that."

What she didn't know was how much more Levi needed to say. But he'd need to time it carefully—for the sake of everyone involved.

~

AN HOUR LATER, Levi took Rebecca to pick up her SUV and then returned to his place. Though Rebecca had enjoyed being around him, she knew he had work to do. She didn't want to keep him from that. Besides, she had a million things on her to-do list.

As she went through some paperwork, she reviewed what Levi had told her. It must've been absolutely devastating for him to find out his wife had been cheating on him. No wonder he got that wistful look in his eyes at times.

It made her respect for him grow even more. He'd also been dealt a hard hand.

Even though just yesterday Rebecca was chiding herself for even considering the idea that the two of them might have a future together, now the possibility seemed more and more intriguing. Was there any chance that the two of them might be able to make something work?

What surprised her even more was the thrill that washed through her at the possibility. She never thought she would be open to the idea of falling in love again. And, though she was a long way away from actually falling in love, the fact that the idea intrigued her was mind-boggling.

She found herself humming as she continued to go through her paperwork. She had one more client she'd been speaking with who might want to see some houses this week. This time, Rebecca would put the proper precautions in place.

While she was thinking about it, she picked up her phone and gave the man a call to firm things up.

"Hi, Abe, this is Rebecca Jarvis. You had talked to me earlier about looking at some houses while you were here in town. I just wanted to follow up."

He cleared his throat. "Hi, Mrs. Jarvis. I'm sorry I didn't get back with you earlier. I hate for you to find out this way, but I actually ended up using Jared Nicholson earlier in the week."

A flash of anger shot through her. Jared? Rebecca knew Jared was new in the area, but she had no idea he would try to steal a client out from beneath her.

"Oh, I see . . ." she finally managed to get out.

"I'm sorry. But I ran into him at a restaurant, and we hit it off. He just drew up an offer for me on a house."

She bit back her disappointment. Having another sale would have done a lot to help her budget. But there was no need to fuss with this man about it. She did, however, plan on talking to Jared.

She thanked Abe and ended the call.

As soon as she put her phone down, it rang again. A number she didn't recognize popped up on the screen. She quickly answered.

A voice she didn't recognize came through the line. "He isn't who he claims to be."

Rebecca froze. Who in the world was this, and what were they talking about? Abe? Jared? "Excuse me?"

"Levi Stoneman. You can't trust him."

And, with that, the line went dead.

CHAPTER EIGHTEEN

BACK AT HIS HOUSE, Levi sat down at his dining room table with a cup of coffee. From here, he had the perfect vantage point to keep an eye on Rebecca's house. If there was trouble, he wanted to know about it. In the meantime, he jotted down notes about everything he'd learned since arriving in Lantern Beach.

Rebecca had two break-ins at her place. Her bank account had been compromised. They'd been chased, and the same car had been driving past Rebecca's place before that.

Jim had been accused of stealing money from his boss. He'd somehow managed to purchase a life insurance policy with Rebecca as the beneficiary,

152

and he'd possibly opened up a secret bank account in Rebecca's name—all without her knowing.

Levi was looking into those things now.

Then there was the man who was arrested yesterday. He must be a member of the Spades, but Levi had never seen him before. He wasn't the leader.

Was more than one person trying to get money from Rebecca? It seemed like a desperate move for the Spades. Then again, they weren't an organization people should mess with. They needed to be brought down.

One thing was becoming more and more clear in his mind: Rebecca was innocent in all of this.

At the thought of her, his heart pounded harder. She really had surprised him. She was smart, capable, and kind. She didn't complain, even though she had every reason to. What was there not to admire about her?

Levi needed to tell her who he really was. Sure, it was against protocol. But they'd begun to trust each other. He couldn't risk Rebecca discovering his true identity any other way. He'd never be able to fix it if she did.

He also needed to come clean with Chief Chambers. The woman knew there was more to Levi than he'd let on. It only made sense to tell her the truth and bring her into his inner circle as well.

His phone rang. It was his boss, Ed, again. A sense of dread fell over Levi as he answered. His new boss was hard-nosed and all business. Ed had spent no time in the field, yet he treated everyone like he was an expert. He was just one more reason why Levi was ready for a career change.

Levi put the phone to his ear. "Ed. What's going on?"

"Two more people are dead."

Levi straightened at the stark words. "What?"

"The Spades are losing it. At least, Black is. He doesn't like to be double-crossed."

That didn't come as a surprise to Levi. Not at all. "The police have one man in custody. He's not talking."

"You need to get him to talk," Ed growled.

"I'm doing my best here. I *am* undercover."

"Did you find any evidence to implicate the wife?"

There Ed went again, calling Rebecca "the wife." It made it a lot less personal that way. But it still rubbed Levi the wrong way. "She's innocent in this."

154

"Just because she's pregnant, don't let that fool you. I heard she was always the brains in the family."

Levi sucked in a breath at the subtle accusation. "You think Rebecca was telling her husband what to do?"

"I'm saying it's a real possibility. That's what I sent you there to find out."

Levi was definitely going to need to look into those bank accounts.

But he still couldn't believe Rebecca would be behind this.

Then again, that was what had gotten him in trouble with Brianna before also. He couldn't let down his guard. Not yet.

That realization pressed heavily on his heart.

REBECCA LEANED BACK in her dining room chair, still trying to process what that caller had told her. Why would someone inform her that Levi wasn't whom he appeared to be? He was an engineer, a man trying still to come to terms with his wife's betrayal.

The man was observant, protective, had a caring

spirit and an almost gentle way. What could he possibly be hiding?

But Rebecca didn't really know that much about him, did she? That was because they'd only known each other a few days. How well could you possibly get to know someone in three days?

She chided herself at the thought.

She froze as a new thought hit her. Her trouble hadn't started until Levi had arrived in town. Was there a connection there that she didn't see?

Rebecca ran a hand through her hair. She didn't know the answer, but the fact that she had even asked that question bothered her on more than one level. Levi had been nothing but kind and compassionate toward her since they met. She had no reason to suspect that he had anything to do with the events of the past few days.

If the intent of that caller had been to shake her up and make her question herself, then it had worked.

Rebecca leaned back and rubbed her stomach again. *Oh, Emma. I already love you so much. I wish I could bring you into this world and always protect you. But that task feels harder and harder every day, and you haven't even been born yet. I'm so sorry for all the times*

I'm going to fail you, but I just want you to know that I already love you.

Less than three weeks until she should arrive. That meant that Rebecca had less than three weeks to get all her affairs in order. Instead of crossing things off, she seemed to be adding things to her to-do list by the bucketful. She still had to drop that death certificate off at Patrick's office, and she wanted to ask Cassidy if she'd located the car whose driver had chased her.

She stared at her phone and tapped the screen.

What was she going to do about Levi? Should she ask him about the phone call? Or, if she did that, would she just be playing into the hands of whoever it was who called her? Then again, if Levi had nothing to hide then it shouldn't hurt to ask that question, right?

Rebecca would have to think about it, she supposed.

For some reason, right now, she had the unquenchable urge to talk to Ron again. What if these crimes were somehow related to Jim's death? What if there was more to the story than Rebecca wanted to acknowledge? Had she stuck her head in the sand for entirely too long?

She hated to admit it, but she thought the answer was yes.

But as the thought settled in her mind, she decided she would go do some errands—starting with Patrick and ending with Ron.

Maybe one of them knew something that she didn't.

158

CHAPTER NINETEEN

AS LEVI CONTINUED to pour over Rebecca's financials, he glanced out his window. A car door opened and then closed. Rebecca had climbed into her SUV.

Where was she going? It wasn't a good idea for her to go anywhere alone.

Surely, she wasn't going to go show another house. Not after what happened yesterday. Or, if she did, certainly she would tell the police so she could have an escort.

Levi considered getting in his car and following her again, but he knew it would be too late by the time he got out there. Besides, if Rebecca caught him following her too often, she would never trust him. Once, she might be able to excuse. But twice? It would just seem creepy.

Despite all his logic, unease continued to jostle inside him. How would Levi ever keep Rebecca safe unless he told her the truth? Telling her the truth could not only harm his investigation, but it was going to further taint her perspective of her late husband, Jim.

Tension pulled across his shoulders.

His computer dinged.

An email from the bank confirmed that Jim had set up a custodial account for Emma before he died.

Levi looked at the amount Jim had deposited.

Five hundred thousand dollars. He blinked. That was no small payout.

Jim must have stolen that money from the Spades. Now they wanted it back. The only way they could get it was through Rebecca—or her child.

A sinking feeling formed in Levi's gut.

Both of their suspicions had been correct—these guys were after Rebecca's money and her child.

But who was behind this? Black probably wouldn't show his face around here. He had henchmen to do his work. One man had already been arrested, but there were others out there.

Most likely, someone else here on the island had taken over for Jim when he died. After all, the Spades would need a contact here. But who?

Jared Nicholson, the competitive realtor? Or how about Ron, the owner of the management company? The man had said his business was on the verge of shutting down. Plus, he would have access to buildings here on the island—buildings needed to smuggle these weapons.

Levi's spine stiffened. He finally felt like he was on to something. Now he needed to figure out his next step.

"REBECCA, what brings you by today? It's always good to see you." Ron stood from his desk and crossed the room to greet her with a hug.

Rebecca paused and shifted uncomfortably in his office doorway.

She had no reason to be uncomfortable. The bad guy was behind bars right now. She should be safe .. . right?

Despite her reassurances, unease jostled inside her. The stress of this week was messing with her mind. She remained by the door, feeling cautious.

"It's good to see you too, Ron. I'm sorry to stop by unannounced."

"You've got to know that you are always welcome

here. Please, have a seat. How is everything going? How's the baby?" He grabbed a mint from a glass dish on his desk and popped one into his mouth.

Emma chose that moment to give another kick. Rebecca tried not to squirm. "She's doing fine. Not much longer and I'll be able to hold her in my arms instead of my belly."

Ron smiled, a family man himself. He had four children, most of whom were teenagers now. "I know you have to be excited. I'm just sorry that Jim is no longer here to share these moments with you."

Rebecca nodded solemnly and decided to sit down in the chair across from Ron's desk. Maybe it would relieve some of the pressure on her back. "Thank you. Me too."

Ron laced his fingers together, and his gaze turned serious. "So what brings you out this way? I figured you would be at home nesting."

"I know this is going to sound weird." Rebecca licked her lips, which were suddenly dry. "But I have a few questions for you, if you don't mind."

"Are you thinking about going into the vacation rental management market?" He raised his eyebrows.

Rebecca let out a chuckle. "No, I'm actually not.

But some strange things have been happening lately, and I wonder if they're somehow tied to Jim."

Ron tilted his head. "What do you mean?"

"I'm realizing that there's so much I don't know about Jim and what he was thinking in the last months before he died. I initially thought his death was an accident and assumed that, before he died, he was having some kind of a midlife crisis. Now I wonder if there's not more to it." Rebecca remained tense. Saying the words out loud hadn't made her feel better. No, it made her feel crazy.

Ron's eyes softened. "I'm not really sure what you want to know. Do you suspect him of doing something illegal?"

"I have no idea. That's why I was hoping you might be able to shed some light on his activities. I know that things ended poorly between the two of you, but I appreciate the fact that you didn't press charges."

"You still don't think that he took that money, huh?" Ron's nose twitched, almost as if he were holding back his true feelings.

Rebecca glanced at her hands, trying to find a truthful answer. She honestly didn't know what the truth was anymore. "I don't want to believe it. I don't want to believe that the man I fell in love with was capable of doing something like that. But I'm starting to question everything."

"He's clearly the one who was most likely to have taken the money. But I always liked Jim. I didn't want to believe he could do it either, which was why I never pressed charges. But you understand that I couldn't let him work here anymore after that trust had been broken."

"Yes, I don't blame you. I would do the same thing in your shoes. I guess I'm just wondering if anything else suspicious happened. I mean, if Jim did take that money, and I'm not saying that he did, I never saw a dime of it. What did he do with it?"

As soon as she said the words, she remembered the life insurance policy that had been set up for her and the bank account. Jim used that stolen money, hadn't he? She didn't want to believe it but . . . it made sense.

"Jim was acting strange the month before all of that happened." Ron rubbed the edge of his desk, his gaze jostling with unease. "I didn't know what was going on with him, if he was just going through a hard time or a midlife crisis. But he wasn't acting like himself. He was quieter, more distant."

"But he never said anything specific?" Rebecca held her breath, hoping for something—anything.

"No, Jim never said anything specific. I do know that he would disappear for periods of time, and he wouldn't be at the location where he was supposed to be."

Ron's words caused Rebecca's spine to tighten. Just where had her husband gone during those times?

She remembered the accusation she'd learned about yesterday. About a house that she represented being involved.

Maybe it was finally time Rebecca did her own investigating. If she didn't find answers, she wasn't sure what the future would hold. But if she looked for answers, she could also be putting herself and her baby in danger.

What was she going to do?

166

CHAPTER TWENTY

REBECCA LEFT Ron and went straight to the police station. She knew this wasn't something she could handle on her own, and she needed to tell Cassidy what was going on.

Cassidy was in her office when Rebecca arrived, and Paige, the dispatcher/receptionist, waved her in. Cassidy's face instantly tensed, as if she was expecting bad news.

"Did something else happen?" Cassidy rushed.

"No, no. I'm sorry to alarm you." She paused across from Cassidy's desk. "Any word on the man you arrested yesterday?"

Cassidy's lips tugged down in a frown as she leaned back in her desk chair. "He hasn't said a word since we arrested him. He refuses to talk."

"That's unfortunate." Rebecca had been hoping for more. "He hasn't even called a lawyer?"

Cassidy crossed her arms and offered a half shrug. "It's funny that you ask that. Because he didn't call a lawyer, but one showed up last night."

"That's curious."

"Isn't it, though?"

"What about the black car whose driver followed me? Any leads?"

Cassidy shook her head. "I wish there were, but there's been nothing. I did track down that FBI agent and we had a fairly lengthy conversation. However, he wasn't very open to telling me all the details."

"Can they do that?"

"Unfortunately, yes." Cassidy paused. "Is that what has brought you by?"

Rebecca rubbed her sweaty hands against her slacks, feeling a rush of nerves. "Actually, I'm here because I'm worried that Jim got himself into some trouble before he died. I've been in denial for a while that something was amiss. I was just trying so hard to concentrate on my pregnancy that I pushed all my concerns aside, thinking it was better for the baby that way. But now everything is coming to the surface, and I realize I should have dealt with this months earlier instead of sticking my head in the sand."

Cassidy tilted her head, her full attention on Rebecca. "What exactly is it that you think is going on?"

Rebecca lowered herself into one of the chairs across from Cassidy.

"I don't know. But I'm starting to wonder if Jim really did take that money from the rental agency when he lost his job." Rebecca's voice cracked.

"Why do you think that?" Cassidy moved to sit in the chair beside Rebecca.

"Because of this savings account that Jim had set up for me. I have no idea where he got the money, but now it's making more and more sense that he may have taken it from Ron. Is there a way to track down those funds and follow the money?"

Cassidy shrugged before shaking her head. "I can look into it and see what I can find out."

"If you wouldn't mind doing that, it would make me feel better. There's no way I'm going to keep any money that is dirty." Rebecca felt sick to her stomach at the thought of it.

Cassidy shifted in her seat, questions brewing in her eyes. "Do you think that's what all of this has been about over the past few days?"

"It's the only thing that makes sense to me. Maybe someone knew that Jim had that money, and they want it." Rebecca didn't want her words to be true, but how could she deny the facts that stared her in the face?

"Wouldn't that point to Ron as the bad guy, though?" Cassidy tilted her head, as if uncertain she was understanding correctly.

"I'm not sure. I don't think Ron is capable of breaking into my house. However, if someone found out Jim stole the money and thinks it's an easy way to get some capital into their own account . . . I don't know. It still doesn't all make sense to me. But I do wonder, if Jim was caught up in something like this, what else he might've been involved in . . ." Nausea churned inside her.

"You mean, you think Jim moved up to Virginia and continued to dig himself into a hole?"

"Yes." The words burned Rebecca's throat. "I hate to even put that theory out there, but it's the only thing that makes sense to me now."

Cassidy offered a compassionate smile. "Thank you for coming forward with this information. I'll see what I can find out."

Rebecca stood. "Thank you."

"I'll let the guys from the FBI know also."

"Good idea."

Before she reached the door, Cassidy called to her. "Rebecca, there's one thing I think you should know."

Rebecca turned toward her, bracing herself for whatever it was she had to say. "Yes?"

Cassidy stood in the door and frowned, questions dancing across her eyes. "I did a little digging into your neighbor."

"Levi?"

"Yes, Levi. It was mostly out of curiosity. It turns out there are some very suspicious holes in his past."

Everything around Rebecca seemed to turn to a dull buzz as Cassidy's words washed over her. Certainly, she'd heard wrong. Or misinterpreted. Or . . . something. "What do you mean?"

Cassidy let out a long breath before saying, "I mean, I can't be sure, but it appears that his identity has been fabricated. I'm sorry, Rebecca."

Rebecca remembered her earlier phone call, the one that said Levi wasn't who he claimed to be.

She felt all of the blood leave her face. What if her knight in shining armor was actually the culprit behind this danger?

∼

LEVI HEARD the car door slam outside. Before he could go to his window to see if Rebecca was back, a knock sounded at the front of his house.

Anticipation spread through him. He hoped it was Rebecca. He'd been thinking about his quandary all morning, and he'd decided to tell her the truth. Tell her who he really was.

When he pulled the door open however, Rebecca stood there with Chief Chambers. Neither of them were happy, based on their narrowed eyes and tight body language.

Apprehension snaked up his spine. They had found out, hadn't they?

Levi didn't bother to fake it. He stepped aside, let them into his home, and shut the door. No one bothered to sit down. Instead, they all stood in the entryway, tension pulled tight between them.

The look in Rebecca's eyes was enough to crush him. Accusation. Hurt. Disappointment. All of it was there.

"Who are you really?" Rebecca demanded, crossing her arms and staring at him.

Levi wanted to deny that he was anyone but Levi Stoneman, but he respected Rebecca too much to do that. "My name really is Levi. But my last name is Marks. I'm Levi Marks."

The chief's hands went to her hips, and she stepped closer to him. "And where are you from, Levi?"

"I really am from Pennsylvania, but I sometimes work in DC."

"Why are you really here?" Rebecca asked. "Are you the one who's been the mastermind behind all the bad things that have happened?"

Levi hated hearing the anger in Rebecca's voice. He'd been the one trying to protect her. Trying to ensure that her stress level was low for the sake of her pregnancy. But he'd brought all this stress on her himself. He hated that fact.

"I can explain." He started to reach for Rebecca but dropped his arm.

Her frosty disposition made it clear that any touch would be rejected. He couldn't blame her. Instead, he shoved his hand into the front pocket of his jeans and tried to relax, to put the women at ease. The task seemed impossible.

Police Chief Chambers continued to stare him down. "Then start talking."

"Would you like to have a seat? It's going to take a minute to explain."

"I have no desire to sit down with someone who has been lying to me for the entire time I have known him." Rebecca's soft accusation was worse than any that could be screamed. The words packed a punch.

"It's not like that." He raised his hands trying to put everyone's emotions at ease. "My name is Levi Marks, and I work for the Department of US Homeland Security. I started as an undercover DEA agent before taking this job and using my connections to help track down weapons smugglers."

Both of the women stared at him, looking like they didn't believe him. He knew it probably sounded like a stretch.

"I was sent here to investigate a gun-running operation. One of the drop-off points appears to be here in Lantern Beach."

The chief put her hands on her hips, her narrowed eyes showing she wasn't happy with his revelation. "If what you're saying is the truth, then why wasn't I informed?"

"Because I'm undercover. That's what I do. I take on new identities in order to find out information."

"And who exactly are you trying to find out information on?" Rebecca's eyes seemed to stare into his soul.

A pit formed in his stomach as he leveled his gaze with hers. "You."

As soon as Levi said the word, he regretted it. Hurt and betrayal washed over Rebecca's features. Hurt and betrayal that he wished he could erase.

"So you were using me this whole time?" Rebecca's voice sounded just above a whisper, and Cassidy touched her arm, as if worried.

"No, I wasn't using you. The things I told you were true. Just not about my job. You've got to understand, I wasn't allowed to share the truth. It was a direct order from my boss that I stay quiet in order to find out information."

"And what exactly are you hoping to find out?" The chief glared at him.

Levi's eyes met Rebecca's. "I needed to find out if Rebecca Jarvis was also involved with her husband's illegal operations."

CHAPTER TWENTY-ONE

LEVI'S WORDS echoed in Rebecca's head until it started pounding. "My husband's illegal gun-running operations?"

Levi nodded, his eyes sympathetic and pleading as they met hers. But Rebecca couldn't trust him anymore. Maybe everything had been a big act. She'd been such a fool.

"We believe that he got mixed up with some people called the Spades," Levi continued. "Jim probably used his rental company connections to provide locations for storing weapons during transport. We also think he got in too deep and wanted out, but it was too late for him to do that."

"So what the FBI said was true?" Rebecca asked.

He nodded.

"And you think I was somehow involved?" Rebecca could hardly believe the words had left her mouth. Why in the world would she be involved with something like that? Then again, how could her husband have been involved? Nothing made sense.

Cassidy turned toward Rebecca, obviously worried about her. "Maybe we should sit down."

Rebecca didn't argue when her friend led her to the dining room table and waited until she was seated. More Braxton Hicks contractions began. Why did they always seem to happen when she was stressed? They were making a bad situation worse.

She took in a deep breath and released it and then repeated. She'd learned the method to keep the pain—and sometimes her panic—under control.

"Do we need to get you to the clinic?" Cassidy placed a hand on her shoulder, her wide eyes worried.

Rebecca shook her head. "No, I'll be fine. I want to hear more. I *need* to hear more."

Levi lowered himself at the table across from her. Her heart pounded with a surprising grief. How could she feel so betrayed by someone she hardly knew? But she understood the answer. Their connection wasn't common. They had bonded quickly and deeply.

She could add that to her list of regrets.

"Rebecca, I never meant to hurt you." Levi's eyes pleaded with her. "I didn't even know who you were when I came here. I just knew that I needed to get information from you so we could track down these guys and stop them. I don't think you realize who we are up against here."

"Why don't you tell us?" Cassidy said.

"These men are putting weapons into the hands of dangerous people. Those people are using them on the streets, and innocent lives are being taken. Two more people have been found dead this week because of the actions of this criminal enterprise."

Rebecca locked gazes with him. "And the story about your wife? Was it real? And the one about your mother having dementia?"

She watched Levi carefully. Emotions clouded his gaze, and he looked down at the table before glancing back up at her. "Yes, it was all true. But there were more details that I didn't tell you. My wife did betray me. She worked for the drug cartel I was trying to bring down. Our relationship was all an act. She was only with me so she could find out information."

A weight formed in Rebecca's heart at the thought of it. Levi may have lied to her about a lot of things, but she felt he was telling the truth right now. She could only imagine the unbearable pain he had gone through.

But this was still so much to comprehend.

"We met in the park when she lost her dog," Levi continued. "I helped her find the poodle, and, before I parted ways, we'd set up a date. I thought she was perfect for me. We were married a year later. But one day, I came home from work early to surprise her. I saw her on my computer. She'd hacked into my work account and was looking at evidence we'd collected. I thought she worked at an art gallery. It turns out, they were using their shipments to hide illegal weapons and sell them."

"Where is she now?" Rebecca asked.

"In jail. For a long time. My testimony put her there." His voice cracked. "She never loved me. It was all an act."

Rebecca didn't know what to say. She could only imagine what he must have felt. Not only had she been betrayed by her husband, but not long ago she'd trusted the wrong people. She'd tried to help a group called Gilead's Cove, only to later find out they were a deadly cult. Thankfully, she'd gotten out before getting involved too deeply.

"What about the FBI?" Cassidy asked. "Why didn't they know you were here?"

"There was a miscommunication. It happens more than it should. They didn't know we were working this case, and I wasn't at liberty to disclose that information. I shouldn't even be talking to you two now."

"So what's next?" Cassidy asked, staring him down.

Levi pressed his lips together in a tight line. "I'm still trying to figure that out. I have a few suspects, but nothing solid yet. All I know is that Rebecca appears to be in danger. Whoever these guys are, they think she's a threat or that she knows something that she doesn't. I only want to keep her safe."

Cassidy didn't break eye contact with him. "You mean that?"

Levi nodded resolutely, leaving no room for doubt. "I do. I'm sorry, Rebecca. I don't know if you'll ever forgive me. But I never expected to meet you and feel the way that I do."

Cassidy glanced at Rebecca before protectively placing an arm around her shoulders. "Maybe I should get you home. This has been a lot."

Rebecca stood. "Yes, I think some time by myself would do me some good."

"Rebecca—" Levi started. His eyes looked apologetic as they glimmered with unspoken emotion.

She raised her hand. "I can't talk any more right now. I just need to think."

Levi opened his mouth as if he might say more but then stopped himself. "I mean it, Rebecca. I never meant to hurt you."

She wanted to believe him, but she just wasn't sure that she could. She'd trusted Jim, and look where it had gotten her. In this mess.

It appeared trusting people was the wrong play to make.

LEVI WATCHED THEM WALK AWAY. Chief Chambers had called over her shoulder that she wanted a word with him—after she walked Rebecca back to her house.

What Levi had feared might happen had happened.

Rebecca would never trust him again, *and* she was in danger.

He rubbed his temples, trying to figure out a way to make this right.

The only way Levi could do that was by keeping her safe. By tracking down whoever was involved in these crimes and arresting him. Then maybe Rebecca could have some peace about the future. Maybe she could live a halfway normal life with Emma here in Lantern Beach.

Because Levi would leave this place. That had been his plan from the start. He'd never intended on staying here.

Then why did his heart feel so attached already?

Levi had no idea. He would finish this assignment . . . and then what? He glanced at the sand dunes in the distance, realizing just how quickly this place had grown on him.

Would he move to DC and start a desk job with Homeland Security? That was the last thing he could envision himself doing. Then *what*?

He didn't have it all figured out yet. He wouldn't for a while.

Levi only knew that the thought of leaving this place did something strange to his heart.

He picked up his phone. He needed more help here. Because something bad was going to go down on Lantern Beach. It would take more than him and

Chief Chambers to put an end to this weapons-smuggling ring.

It was going to get uglier before it got better.

Cassidy appeared back at his door, looking all business. Any of the comradery they'd shared earlier was gone.

"I want your badge number," she said.

"Of course." He recited it to her, watching as she jotted it down on a pad of paper.

"I should have been informed. I'm in charge of keeping this island safe."

"It wasn't my choice." He glanced beyond Cassidy and saw Rebecca pulling out. "Where is she going?"

"She's going by her office for a moment. Don't worry—one of my officers is going to follow her." The chief shifted. "Do you know anything about the house on Coastal Shores?"

"Only what you know. The FBI must have other intel."

She gave him a look.

Levi raised his hands. "I promise."

"Anything else I should know?"

Levi watched as Rebecca's SUV pulled away before turning his gaze back to Chambers. "We believe that an out-of-towner would be too suspicious here on the island at this time of year. In other words, we believe a local is involved in this operation —someone who took Jim's place."

"Who?"

Levi shrugged. "That's the kicker. We haven't been able to figure it out."

CHAPTER TWENTY-TWO

AFTER REBECCA LEFT LEVI'S, she climbed into her SUV and slammed the door. Cassidy had walked her out and did a mental health check on her.

Rebecca assured her friend that she was okay and just needed time to process everything. She planned on swinging by her office. It would help her keep her mind occupied. The last thing she wanted was to stay at the house thinking about Levi's betrayal.

As she traveled down the road, Rebecca glanced in the rearview mirror and confirmed that Officer Banks was following her in the patrol vehicle. She did find some comfort in knowing he was there, even if he did look like he was just out of high school.

Her mind still spun from everything she'd learned. Not only was her late husband a criminal, but the new guy that Rebecca had started falling for had been lying to her. Man, did she know how to pick them.

Rebecca glanced quickly at her belly. "Maybe you can learn from all my mistakes, baby Emma. Hopefully, you won't inherit your mom's naivety."

As Rebecca headed toward the business district on the island, her gaze wandered to some of the original buildings here on Lantern Beach. Her dad had owned one of the fish-processing plants here. When he retired, he'd tried to sell it, but they hadn't found any buyers.

She'd just come across a picture of her and Dad in front of that building when she'd been picking up everything after her place had been ransacked. When she remembered how much she'd shared with Levi, her heart sagged again.

She'd been so stupid to trust him. So, so stupid. But it was too late to go back now.

On a whim, she pulled into the lot and put her SUV in Park. She knew this was probably nothing, but she had seen Jim leaving this building one time. She had asked him about it, and he said he had just taken some time to clear his head.

Before he'd left her, he'd been prone to fishing and spending a lot of time alone. Rebecca hadn't thought that much of it at the time. Or, then again, maybe she'd simply stuck her head in the sand and not wanted to acknowledge the truth.

She climbed from her SUV and pulled her coat closer as a chilly wind pierced the air. Droplets of rain felt like little knives as they hit her skin. She jogged over to Officer Banks's car and knocked on his window. He rolled it down and squinted against the precipitation that speckled his car.

"I'm going to run inside my dad's old building for a minute. I just wanted to let you know."

He turned toward the metal-sided building. "Do you want me to go with you?"

Rebecca glanced around. There were no other cars in the area. For that matter, there were no other cars on the road. She should be fine. She'd only be inside for a moment.

"No, just give me a minute."

He nodded and rolled his window back up.

She hurried to the door. She always carried a key to this building with her. She'd briefly put it on the market and, as a result, carried a skeleton key.

Quickly, she unlocked the dingy building and stepped inside. Darkness surrounded her, as well as the scent of fish. Just being here brought back memories from her childhood—memories of helping her dad, of waiting for him to return home after long jaunts at sea. But she didn't have time to dwell on them now.

Rebecca didn't really know what she was doing here, but something internal had led her to this place. Maybe it was just curiosity. Maybe she needed to put her mind at ease. But what if her husband had used this facility in his exploits?

Maybe she should call Cassidy.

No, not yet. Besides, Banks was outside.

Instinctively, Rebecca reached for the light switch, but nothing happened. Of course. The power had been turned off. She could barely pay the electric bill for her own home, so no way would she waste her money to sustain this one. However, it was awfully dark.

She pulled up a flashlight app on her phone and shined it around. The inside of the place looked just as Rebecca remembered it, save for a few critters that had taken up residence here. There were tables where crab meat had been processed and where clams and oysters had been cleaned before being shipped out to market.

She walked across the building to the double doors on the other side. This side backed up to the harbor area, and sometimes Rebecca was still surprised that no one had ever purchased the building. But it would be the perfect place to do something secretive since it was out of sight from most of the other buildings.

She opened the massive doors, and light flooded inside. Instantly, her mind was at ease.

Feeling better, Rebecca scanned the place one more time. She didn't see anything out of the ordinary. It didn't look like anyone had been here for a long time, for that matter.

She walked along the perimeter one more time, and then she decided she would leave for her office. As she reached the other side of the building, something on the floor caught her eye.

While most of the place was dusty and dank, right here it looked like something had been slid along the floor. Something large. Maybe some boxes?

Boxes full of . . . guns?

Her instincts went on alert. Maybe her husband had been involved in what he had been accused of. And maybe this was the source of his operations.

She had to tell Cassidy. And maybe Levi too. But as she turned to do so, she heard a footfall behind her.

It looked like she was too late.

CHAPTER TWENTY-THREE

LEVI FELT BESIDE HIMSELF. Not only had he ruined things with Rebecca, but he knew she was in danger. It would be harder to protect her now that she didn't trust him.

But that didn't mean he was going to stop trying.

Spontaneously, he grabbed his car keys. He knew how it would look if he went after Rebecca. But they needed to talk, and she needed someone to keep an eye on her. Her well-being was more important than their relationship at this point—although Levi did hope he could restore the beginnings of the relationship that had started this week.

He would head out and look for her.

As he rushed to his car, he lifted up a prayer that nothing had happened to her.

194

Rebecca had no idea what kind of men they were dealing with. These guys, the Spades, were dangerous. Levi wasn't even sure that Chief Chambers fully understood just how bad these people were.

The Spades thought that Rebecca had something they wanted, and they weren't going to stop until they got it back. That put Rebecca in a very bad place right now.

Levi continued cruising the road, glancing down the side streets and hoping to spot Rebecca's SUV. Maybe she had gone to her office like the chief said. That would make the most sense.

He headed in that direction, still keeping his eyes open.

But, outside her building, he still didn't see Rebecca's SUV. He pulled into the small parking area and paused. Where in the world could she have gone?

A bad feeling grew in his stomach. He swallowed his pride and picked up his phone. First, he dialed Rebecca's number. She didn't answer. Next, he dialed the police station. A moment later, he was patched through to Chief Chambers.

"Chief, this is Levi. I know I'm not your favorite person right now, but I'm looking for Rebecca."

"She went into the office for a little while. I have an officer with her."

"I'm at her office right now, and there is no one here."

Chambers paused for a moment. "Did you try her phone?"

"She didn't answer."

"I'll call Banks and put an APB out for her if I need to."

"Thanks, Chief."

"We need to find her," Chambers said.

"I know. Believe me. You might not think much of me right now, but I really do care about Rebecca."

"I think you messed up, but let's see if we can make all of this right."

He ended the call and put his car in Drive. He was going to search every last inch of this island until he found Rebecca. If it was the last thing he did.

REBECCA SLOWLY TURNED AROUND until she saw . . . Patrick Peterson standing there.

"Patrick? You're involved in this." How in the

world had Mr. Boring gotten mixed up in this? If anyone, she thought maybe Jared, but . . . Patrick?

He offered a half-hearted shrug as he raised the gun in his hands. His eyes almost looked glazed, but his hands were shaky, as if anxiety quelled inside him. "It's complicated, but let's just say my attention to detail has served me well. Or, at least, it's served the Spades well."

"Why would you do this?" Rebecca blinked, nearly certain this was just a bad dream. And where was Banks? Why wasn't he rushing inside to help right now?

"It's a long story. But once these people pull you in, it's nearly impossible to get out."

"Is that what happened with Jim?" The facts spun in Rebecca's head, and she desperately tried to make sense of them. But the overall picture that tried to form wasn't one she was prepared to accept. However, she had no choice. She had to know the truth.

"It is. He saw a way of making a few quick bucks. But then there was no way for him to return to normal life. They hold what you do against you in order to make you continue to do their dirty work." Sweat beaded across his skin, all the way from his cheeks to the top of his partially bald head.

"Jim's death wasn't an accident at all, was it?"
Come on, Banks. I need your help. Now!

Patrick shook his head, his breaths coming more quickly. "No, it wasn't. I'm going to be next. Now, you have something I need."

"I have no idea what that might be. Believe me, after everything that's happened this week, I've given this plenty of thought."

"Jim took some money from us, and we need it back. If I don't get it, they're going to kill me." The gun trembled in his hand as Patrick aimed it at her chest.

"Was this money related to the life insurance policy?"

"No, that was different. I don't know where he got that money. But he stole from the men we work for. He intercepted one of the weapons shipments and decided to sell them himself. He walked away with nearly five hundred thousand dollars from that."

Rebecca sucked in a breath. "Five hundred thousand? That's a lot of money."

"No joke." His voice cracked. "I need you to help me get it back."

She took a step backward, looking around for something to use to defend herself. A rusty clam

rake leaned against the wall. If only she could grab it
. . .

She glanced at Patrick. "How am I supposed to help you get it back?"

"We believe that he set up a custodial fund for your daughter. We need you to get into that fund and hand the money over to us."

That email Levi had found wasn't a scam. This was bigger than Rebecca had ever thought. "But I don't want that money. All you had to do was ask, and I would have given it to you."

"You would've turned us in." Patrick's face reddened. "Please, Rebecca. Help me get it back before they kill me too. Please don't make this any harder. I don't want to hurt you. I really don't."

As he said the words, a contraction hit her. Rebecca nearly doubled over as her muscles tightened. Braxton Hicks? She wasn't sure.

"You're not having the baby, are you?" His eyes widened.

Rebecca squeezed her eyes shut, in no position right now to grab a makeshift weapon. "I don't know what's going on. But it doesn't feel good."

"Rebecca . . ." Patrick stared at her a moment and then it almost looked like something snapped inside him. He drew in a deep breath, as if drawing on some inner strength. "You're going to have to wait on delivering your baby. Because before anything else happens, I need the money."

She glanced at the door, still hoping that Banks would rush inside.

Patrick seemed to read her thoughts, and he grabbed her arm, pulling her closer. "Don't worry about the officer outside. I already knocked him out. I didn't want to, but I had no other choice. I'm in this deep, Rebecca. Too deep."

Another tremble of fear went through Rebecca. This man was desperate, there was no doubt about that. His desperation made him unpredictable. He just might carry through on his threats.

She swallowed hard and kept her voice even as she asked, "What do I need to do?"

"I need to take you to the bank, and I need you to act like everything is normal as you transfer the money over to me." His gun jammed into her side.

Another contraction hit her, and a groan escaped from her lips. "I'm not going to make it to the mainland to a bank."

"Rebecca . . . don't do this to me." Patrick gripped her arm tighter until she nearly cried out.

How had he gotten himself into this mess? No wonder he'd been hounding her about that policy.

He'd also asked her which account the funds should be deposited in. He'd been fishing for information, hadn't he?

Rebecca glanced out the door. Banks was slumped over the steering wheel of his police cruiser. Nobody else knew she was here.

Another contraction hit her. Rebecca closed her eyes.

Dear Lord, what am I going to do?

CHAPTER TWENTY-FOUR

LEVI HAD GONE from one end of the island to the next, and he hadn't found Rebecca.

She had to be here somewhere. He kept moving down the highway, his thoughts racing. Where might she be?

He had no idea.

He searched his memories for all the conversations they'd had. Were there any that might indicate where she would have gone?

His mind fast-forwarded through the pictures he'd seen at Rebeca's place. There had been one of Rebecca with her father down by the water. It had looked like a more commercial area.

My dad used to own a seafood-processing facility . . .

Knowing how sentimental Rebecca was, what if she'd held on to it?

Levi had no idea if she had or not, but it was worth a try. Levi had seen a more commercial area near the harbor. He headed there now.

Ten minutes later, he reached the harbor. He slowed as his gaze scanned the buildings there.

Finally, his perusal stopped on a burgundy SUV. It was Rebecca's. A police car was parked behind it, and someone appeared to be inside.

Levi pulled his car behind the building, just to be safe, and hopped out.

Creeping along the wall, he reached the corner and eyeballed the police cruiser there. The officer was slumped over the steering wheel.

Concern surged through him. He pulled out his phone and dialed the chief's number.

"We have an officer down at the harbor," Levi said. "We need back-up. Now."

"Where's Rebecca?" the chief rushed.

"I'm nearly certain she's inside her father's old processing plant."

"I'm on my way."

Putting away his phone, Levi drew his gun and stepped toward the metal-sided building. Voices drifted from inside. Who was that with Rebecca? He wasn't sure, but this wasn't good. One of the Spades had found her.

"I'm not going to make it to the mainland to a bank," Rebecca said.

To the mainland? Someone wanted to take her off of the island? That was a bad, bad idea.

Suddenly, she let out a yell.

Levi's muscles tightened. Had the man hurt her?

He didn't think so. That almost sounded like . . . she was going into labor.

Levi sucked in a tight breath. He knew he didn't have much time. He needed to act, and he needed to do it now.

He remained by the edge of the door as he heard her getting closer. As soon as two figures stepped out, Levi pointed his gun at them. Rebecca gasped. The next instant, the man had his gun to her temple.

"One move and she dies," the man growled.

Patrick Peterson, Levi realized. He'd looked up his picture online as soon as he heard about her life insurance.

Patrick had been behind this the whole time. Levi's suspicion that a local was involved was correct.

"You don't want to hurt Rebecca," Levi said. "We can get you the money without anyone being harmed."

Sweat spread across Patrick's forehead. "You don't understand. I'm a dead man if I don't get that money."

"You're going to be a dead man if you hurt Rebecca. You need to let her go." Levi kept his gun raised. If he saw the man start to pull the trigger, Patrick was going down. Levi hoped it didn't come to that.

"I knew you were up to no good. I tried to warn you, Rebecca," Patrick said.

"You were the one who made that call?" she gasped.

"He messed up all my plans." Patrick's breathing became heavier, more desperate.

Rebecca let out another cry, and her hand went to her lower abdomen.

"Rebecca?" Concern ricocheted through Levi.

"I think the baby is coming." Her voice turned thin. "These are real contractions."

Concern rose in Levi. Rebecca didn't need to be here. She certainly didn't need that gun pointed at her head. But the situation was precarious, and he needed to figure out the best way to get her out of it.

Cassidy and her crew should be here any minute. Until then, he needed to keep Patrick talking.

"There's a better way," Levi said. "You can help the police, and you can put the rest of these guys behind bars."

"They would kill me before I could do that." Patrick's voice quivered, and he glanced around.

"We could protect you. I work with Homeland Security. I have connections. We can put you in Witness Protection."

"They would find me." More sweat beaded on his forehead, despite the frigid temperatures.

"No, they wouldn't. You give us the names, and I'll make sure that you're safe. I just need you to put the gun down."

Rebecca let out another cry. The contractions were coming faster, and her face looked pale. She was going to deliver this baby. Soon, if Levi had to guess.

Patrick shook his head quickly, as if his thoughts were driving him mad. "I can't let her go. She is my only leverage."

"Listen to me, Patrick. There are other ways. You have got to trust me."

"I never wanted to get mixed up in this."

"And this is your chance to make things right."

Patrick didn't say anything. He almost looked as if he was contemplating what to do. Levi prayed he'd make the right decision. More than anything, Levi wanted Rebecca by his side right now. He wanted to know that she and Emma would be safe and protected.

At that moment, another car pulled onto the scene. Except it wasn't Chief Chambers. It was the Spades, Levi realized.

Things had just gotten ten times worse.

REBECCA MOANED as another pain shot through her abdomen. She thought she might throw up. Her baby was coming. And she was coming soon.

She watched as two men with guns climbed from the other vehicle, and she bit back a cry. This wasn't good. There was no way Levi could protect her from so many people.

Patrick shoved the barrel of his gun into her side harder until she let out another yelp. One slip of his finger, and Rebecca would be a goner.

The two men surrounded them, each wearing black masks and holding guns. Levi's weapon remained on Patrick—and Rebecca had a feeling it would as long as the man had Rebecca in his grasp.

"Where is our money?" one of the men asked.

"I'll get it for you," Patrick said.

"That's not good enough. We gave you a day. It's been three. I would say we have been plenty gracious."

"No, I will. I promise!" Patrick said.

"Black knew you were weak," one of the men said. "That's why he sent Jenkins—to do what you couldn't. When breaking into her house didn't work, he planned on forcing her to talk while looking at real estate."

That hadn't gotten Black very far then. Jenkins was now behind bars. Rebecca kept the thought to herself.

But that made sense. She couldn't see Patrick doing those things. He'd tried for a subtle approach.

Another contraction hit, and Rebecca tried to bite back a cry. It didn't work. The pain in her abdomen was growing. At once, she felt something shift inside her and gasped.

"My water. It broke."

At her pronouncement, every man seemed to go pale. But no one lowered their weapons.

"We can get you what you want," Levi said, suddenly looking as tough as she'd envisioned him being. She kind of liked this side of him. "You just need to let Rebecca go."

"She's not going anywhere," one of the men—the louder of the two—said. "She's coming with us. Her and her baby too. She's our key to getting the money back. Her husband double-crossed us, and now someone has to pay."

"There's no need to make someone innocent pay. She didn't do anything, and neither did her baby."

"Put her in the car," the man ordered.

In the car? No . . . !

She glanced at Levi, and his gaze mirrored hers. He knew only bad things would happen if she got in that vehicle.

Despite everything that had happened between them, she knew he was a good guy. He'd only been trying to bring down a deadly criminal organization.

She prayed they would have a chance to have more conversations. Seeing how he was putting his life on the line for her now did something strange to her heart.

Patrick hesitated for a moment. His fingers dug into Rebecca's arm. He drew in a deep breath before nodding and pulling her away.

No . . .

He was going to do it. Going to send her off with these thugs.

She might not ever see this island again.

As her muscles tightened, Rebecca nearly doubled over.

"Don't do this!" Levi called. "There are other ways."

"Like what?" one of the men asked.

"Take me instead. I'll help you find what you need."

Levi . . . he couldn't do that. He couldn't offer up himself for her. These men would torture and kill him.

"No, Levi," she whispered, almost at the car now.

She wanted to fight back . . . but the pain in her abdomen consumed her. Didn't allow her to do anything else except feel.

"I'm sorry, Rebecca," Levi said. "For everything."

She wanted to respond, to reassure him, to . . . somehow make things right. If that was possible.

Before she could say or do anything, Levi sprang into action. He tackled one of the gunmen and grabbed the man's weapon before putting him on the ground. As the second man came at him, Levi swung his leg.

The man's gun skittered across the pavement. Before the man could grab it again, Levi raised his weapon. "I wouldn't do that."

Rebecca drew in a deep breath. In and out. In and out. Trying to control her pain.

Patrick still held the gun to her side.

This wasn't over yet.

Just as the thought entered her head, more men surrounded them. "FBI!"

FBI? Rebecca glanced around. Saw the letters on the men's vests.

Cassidy and two of her officers also arrived, weapons drawn and ready to take action.

Patrick lowered his gun to the ground and raised his hands in the air.

"I'm so sorry, Rebecca." His voice broke. "I never wanted to do any of this. I got in too deep. I didn't really want to hurt you."

She started to reply when another contraction hit her. She held her stomach and bent over. A deep moan escaped from her lips.

Patrick was the least of her concerns at the moment.

This baby was coming.

Soon.

LEVI SAW Rebecca double over with pain. He heard her moan.

She needed help. Now.

He handed the confiscated weapons to one of the FBI agents and jogged over to her. Chief Chambers stood with her now, talking in low tones.

"Let me take her to the hospital," Levi said. "Please."

Chief Chambers gave him a look that clearly said she was still leery of him. "That's up to Rebecca."

He turned to her as paramedics nudged her onto a stretcher. "Rebecca—"

She grabbed his hand, her eyes squeezing shut. "Yes."

"Yes what?"

"Yes, you can come with me."

Levi let out a shaky breath. She hadn't pushed him away. Maybe there was a possibility she'd forgive him. He could pray that was the case. He never wanted his job to come between them again.

Chief Chambers shot him a warning glance before nodding. "Keep an eye on her."

"I will." He climbed into the back of the ambulance with Rebecca. Two paramedics hooked her up to an IV while taking her pulse. Levi didn't let go of

225

her hand as his heart thumped nervously in his chest.

He was probably more nervous about this than he'd been facing those gunman.

Rebecca groaned and held her stomach. Her eyes squeezed shut before she released several quick, controlled breaths.

"It's going to be okay," Levi murmured.

Rebecca was going to have a baby. Emma was going to make her entrance into the world. He only hoped the baby would wait until they arrived at the clinic.

"Nothing feels okay." Her voice came out in a low moan, followed by more controlled breathing.

"I'm sorry, Rebecca." How could Levi ever make this up to her? He'd done so much damage . . . damage that he wasn't sure he could make right.

"I'm . . . sorry . . . too. I just . . . wish you'd . . . told me . . ." She breathed deeply and moaned between every other word.

"I wanted to. I really did. I never expected to feel this way about you."

The ambulance siren wailed as they took off.

"How . . . do . . . you . . . feel?" Her moan turned into a near scream.

Levi's heart thumped harder and harder. "Like I'm falling in love."

Rebecca's grip on his hand tightened until pain ripped through his fingers. He said nothing.

"You saved my life. I guess . . . I can . . ." A smile started on her face, but abruptly disappeared as another half-moan, half-scream escaped from her.

"This baby is coming," the paramedic said. "Call the clinic. Make sure Doc Clemson is ready. We don't have a lot of time."

Levi prayed that everything would be all right. What was Rebecca about to say? He supposed it could wait.

He only hoped that at the end of this, she didn't hate him. But his deepest wish was that she would allow Levi to be a part of her life. Was he hoping for the impossible? Had he messed up beyond the point of forgiveness?

Sweat covered Rebecca's face, and her cries of pain came more rapidly.

"Contractions are only thirty seconds apart," the paramedic said. "We don't have much time."

They pulled up to the clinic. Before the paramedics took the stretcher out, Rebecca squeezed Levi's hand. Her gaze met his, and, for a brief moment, her pain seemed to clear.

214

"I forgive you," she whispered.

Relief greater than any he'd ever felt before washed through Levi. "Thank you, Rebecca."

"No, thank you."

With those final words, the medics took her away.

Levi remained in the waiting room. He paced, feeling more nervous than a first-time father. This baby wasn't his. He knew that.

But he also knew it was his duty to watch out for both Rebecca and Emma.

He had no doubt about that.

CHAPTER TWENTY-FIVE

SIX MONTHS LATER

REBECCA PLACED a pearl earring in her ear and glanced in the mirror. They used to belong to her mother.

She smiled at her reflection there.

She'd been so uncertain if she'd be able to handle being a single working mom.

The past several months hadn't always been easy, but she'd managed to make it through.

With one more glance, she felt satisfied she looked okay. She walked to the crib nestled in her bedroom and smiled at the baby there.

Emma Jarvis was perfect in every way. As the baby played with her toes and drool escaped from her mouth, Rebecca's heart melted a little more.

How did Rebecca deserve to be this incredibly

2.16

blessed? She didn't deserve it, but she was so thankful for the way her life had turned around.

As her doorbell rang, she scooped Emma up in her arms and walked downstairs. When she opened the door, her breath caught.

Levi stood there. Levi Marks.

He grinned as he leaned forward to kiss her cheek. "Good evening."

She felt herself glowing. "Good evening."

He stepped inside and put a hand on Emma's back. Emma's face seemed to glow when she spotted him also.

"How's my little girl doing?" Levi asked, leaning closer.

Emma reached for him, and Levi lifted the baby into his arms. The two seemed attached at the hip sometimes. It was a good thing Levi was still renting the house next door.

"Thanks for staying in for our date tonight." Rebecca shut the door and joined them in the entryway. "All the restaurants are just going to be so busy with tourist season in full swing."

"I prefer staying in to fighting the crowds." He made another face at Emma, and the baby smiled, blowing a raspberry.

The sight warmed Rebecca's heart. She loved watching the two of them together.

Levi had decided to stay in Lantern Beach. He'd given up his job with Homeland Security, and he was now working as a consultant with the government. The arrangement was working great—for now, at least.

Things had really turned around in the past few months. That money that Jim had left Rebecca had been dirty. Part of it had been Ron's, and, after a long process, he'd been paid back. His business had been able to stay open.

Apparently, Jim had stolen that money in desperation. In the meantime, he'd found himself in over his head with the Spades—and he wanted out. From what Patrick had told Cassidy, Jim moved away to keep Rebecca safe. But he hated what he was doing.

Eventually, he stole money from the Spades and put it into a savings account, hoping it would ultimately help Rebecca and the baby. The Spades discovered what he'd done, and they'd killed him. They'd come to Lantern Beach, trying to figure out what Jim had done with their money.

Jim's intentions might have been good, but his

218

methods left a lot to be desired. There was no way Rebecca could keep that money. She didn't want it.

Three members of the Spades, including Patrick, had been arrested. There were more out there, but the arm that operated in North Carolina had been shut down. It would be an ongoing process, for sure. At least, it was behind them now.

"Rebecca?" Levi asked.

She wandered into the kitchen toward the stove. She'd put some shrimp alfredo in the oven earlier. She'd been lost in her thoughts as she pulled it out and hadn't heard Levi say her name until he repeated it again.

"Yes?" She turned toward him as he stood behind her, with Emma in his arms. He'd never looked more appealing.

She sucked in a breath when she saw the object in his hands.

A ring.

"Rebecca, I was going to wait until after dinner, but I don't want to wait a moment longer," Levi started. "As you can see, you and Emma have quickly gained a place in my heart. Nothing would make me happier than if you'd become my wife and if Emma would allow me to be her father."

Tears rushed to Rebecca's eyes. She didn't even

have to think about her response. "Yes! Yes, we'd love that too, Levi!"

He slipped the ring onto her finger, and her breath caught when she saw the diamond there. The princess-cut stone was beautiful.

Things had progressed so well over the last six months. He'd been there for her at every turn and had proven he could be trusted.

Their gazes caught, and they stepped closer to each other. Rebecca reached up, and her hand skimmed his beard. "I love you, Levi Marks."

A grin stretched across his lips. "I love you too, Rebecca Jarvis. And you, little Emma."

Their lips met in a warm kiss . . . that was only interrupted by Emma's babbling and eventually her chubby hand as it came between them.

They stepped back and chuckled.

Against all the odds, Rebeca finally had the family she'd always dreamed about.

ALSO BY CHRISTY BARRITT:

murder investigation, she can't resist stepping in. But Cassidy is supposed to be keeping a low profile. One wrong move could lead to both her discovery and her demise. Can she bring justice to the island ... or will the hidden currents surrounding her pull her under for good?

Flood Watch

The tide is high, and so is the danger on Lantern Beach. Still in hiding after infiltrating a dangerous gang, Cassidy Livingston just has to make it a few more months before she can testify at trial and resume her old life. But trouble keeps finding her, and Cassidy is pulled into a local investigation after a man mysteriously disappears from the island she now calls home. A recurring nightmare from her time undercover only muddies things, as does a visit from the parents of her handsome ex-Navy SEAL neighbor. When a friend's life is threatened, Cassidy must make choices that put her on the verge of blowing her cover. With a flood watch on her emotions and her life in a tangle, will Cassidy find the truth? Or will her past finally drown her?

Storm Surge

A storm is brewing hundreds of miles away, but its effects are devastating even from afar. Laid-back, loose, and light: that's Cassidy Livingston's new motto. But when a makeshift boat with a bloody cloth inside washes ashore near her oceanfront home, her detective instincts shift into gear . . . again. Seeking clues isn't the only thing on her mind—romance is heating up with next-door neighbor and former Navy SEAL Ty Chambers as well. Her heart wants the love and stability she's longed for her entire life. But her hidden identity only leads to a tidal wave of turbulence. As more answers emerge about the boat, the danger around her rises, creating a treacherous swell that threatens to reveal her past. Can Cassidy mind her own business, or will the storm surge of violence and corruption that has washed ashore on Lantern Beach leave her life in wreckage?

Dangerous Waters

Danger lurks on the horizon, leaving only two choices: find shelter or flee. Cassidy Livingston's new identity has begun to feel as comfortable as her favorite sweater. She's been tucked away on Lantern Beach for weeks, waiting to testify against a deadly gang, and is settling in to a new life she wants to last forever. When she thinks she spots someone malevolent from her past, panic swells inside her. If an enemy has found her, Cassidy won't be the only one who's a target. Everyone she's come to love will also be at risk. Dangerous waters threaten to pull her into an overpowering chasm she may never escape. Can Cassidy survive what lies ahead? Or has the tide fatally turned against her?

Perilous Riptide

Just when the current seems safer, an unseen danger emerges and threatens to destroy everything. When Cassidy Livingston finds a journal hidden deep in the recesses of her ice cream truck, her curiosity kicks into high gear. Islanders suspect that Elsa, the journal's owner, didn't die accidentally. Her final entry indicates their suspicions might be correct and that what Elsa observed on her final night may have led to her demise. Against the advice of Ty Chambers, her former Navy SEAL boyfriend, Cassidy taps into her detective skills and hunts for answers. But her search only leads to a skeletal body and trouble for both of them. As helplessness threatens to drown her, Cassidy is desperate to turn back time. Can Cassidy find what she needs to navigate the perilous situation? Or will the riptide surrounding her threaten everyone and everything Cassidy loves?

Deadly Undertow

The current's fatal pull is powerful, but so is one detective's will to live. When someone from Cassidy Livingston's past shows up on Lantern Beach and warns her of impending peril, opposing currents collide, threatening to drag her under. Running would be easy. But leaving would break her heart. Cassidy must decipher between the truth and lies, between reality and deception. Even more importantly, she must decide whom to trust and whom to fear. Her life depends on it. As danger rises and answers surface, everything Cassidy thought she knew is tested. In order to survive, Cassidy must take drastic measures and end the battle against the ruthless gang DH-7 once and for all. But if her final mission fails, the consequences will be as deadly as the raging undertow.

LANTERN BEACH ROMANTIC SUSPENSE

Tides of Deception

Change has come to Lantern Beach: a new police chief, a new season, and . . . a new romance? Austin

Brooks has loved Skye Lavinia from the moment they met, but the walls she keeps around her seem impenetrable. Skye knows Austin is the best thing to ever happen to her. Yet she also knows that if he learns the truth about her past, he'd be a fool not to run. A chance encounter brings secrets bubbling to the surface, and danger soon follows. Are the life-threatening events plaguing them really accidents . . . or is someone trying to send a deadly message? With the tides on Lantern Beach come deception and lies. One question remains—who will be swept away as the water shifts? And will it bring the end for Austin and Skye, or merely the beginning?

Shadow of Intrigue

For her entire life, Lisa Garth has felt like a supporting character in the drama of life. The desig-nation never bothered her—until now. Lantern Beach, where she's settled and runs a popular restaurant, has boarded up for the season. The slower pace leaves her with too much time alone. Braden Dillinger came to Lantern Beach to try to heal. The former Special Forces officer returned from battle with invisible scars and diminished hope. But his recovery is hampered by the fact that an unknown enemy is trying to kill him. From the moment Lisa and Braden meet, danger ignites around them, and both are drawn into a web of intrigue that turns their lives upside down. As shadows creep in, will Lisa and Braden be able to shine a light on the peril around them? Or will the encroaching darkness turn their worst nightmares into reality?

Storm of Doubt

A pastor who's lost faith in God. A romance writer who's lost faith in love. A faceless man with a deadly obsession. Nothing has felt right in Pastor Jack Wilson's world since his wife died two years ago. He hoped coming to Lantern Beach might help soothe the ragged edges of his soul. Instead, he feels more alone than ever. Novelist Juliette Grace came to the island to hide away. Though her professional life has never been better, her personal life has imploded. Her husband left her and a stalker's threats have grown more and more dangerous. When Jack saves Juliette from an attack, he sees the terror in her gaze and knows he must protect her. But when danger strikes again, will Jack be able to keep her safe? Or will the approaching storm prove too strong to withstand?

Winds of Danger

Wes O'Neill is perfectly content to hang with his friends and enjoy island life on Lantern Beach. Something begins to change inside him when Paige Henderson sweeps into his life. But the beautiful newcomer is hiding painful secrets beneath her cheerful facade. Police dispatcher Paige Henderson came to Lantern Beach riddled with guilt and uncertainties after the fallout of a bad relationship. When she meets Wes, she begins to open up to the possibility of love again. But there's something Wes isn't telling her—something that could change everything. As the winds shift, doubts seep into Paige's mind. Can Paige and Wes trust each other, even as the currents work against them? Or is trouble from the past too much to overcome?

LANTERN BEACH PD

On the Lookout

When Cassidy Chambers accepted the job as police chief on Lantern Beach, she knew the island had its secrets. But a suspicious death with potentially far-reaching implications will test all her skills —and threaten to reveal her true identity. Cassidy enlists the help of her husband, former Navy SEAL

Ty Chambers. As they dig for answers, both uncover parts of their pasts that are best left buried. Not everything is as it seems, and they must figure out if their John Doe is connected to the secretive group that has moved onto the island. As facts materialize, danger on the island grows. Can Cassidy and Ty discover the truth about the shadowy crimes in their cozy community? Or has darkness permanently invaded their beloved Lantern Beach?

Attempt to Locate

A fun girls' night out turns into a nightmare when armed robbers barge into the store where Cassidy and her friends are shopping. As the situation escalates and the men escape, a massive manhunt launches on Lantern Beach to apprehend the dangerous trio. In the midst of the chaos, a potential foe asks for Cassidy's help. He needs to find his sister who fled from the secretive Gilead's Cove community on the island. But the more Cassidy learns about the seemingly untouchable group, the more her unease grows. The pressure to solve both cases continues to mount. But as the gravity of the situation rises, so does the danger. Cassidy is determined to protect the island and break up the cult . . . but doing so might cost her everything.

First Degree Murder

Police Chief Cassidy Chambers longs for a break from the recent crimes plaguing Lantern Beach. She simply wants to enjoy her friends' upcoming wedding, to prepare for the busy tourist season about to slam the island, and to gather all the dirt she can on the suspicious community that's invaded the town. But trouble explodes on the island, sending residents—including Cassidy—into a squall of uneasiness. Cassidy may have more than one enemy plotting her demise, and the collateral damage seems unthinkable. As the temperature rises, so does the pressure to find answers. Someone is determined that Lantern Beach would be better off without their new police chief. And for Cassidy, one wrong move could mean certain death.

Dead on Arrival

With a highly charged local election consuming the community, Police Chief Cassidy Chambers braces herself for a challenging day of breaking up petty conflicts and tamping down high emotions. But when widespread food poisoning spreads among potential voters across the island, Cassidy smells something rotten in the air. As Cassidy examines every possibility to uncover what's going on, local enigma Anthony Gilead again comes on her radar. The man is running for mayor and his cult-like following is growing at an alarming rate. Cassidy feels certain he has a spy embedded in her inner circle. The problem is that her pool of suspects gets deeper every day. Can Cassidy get to the bottom of what's eating away at her peaceful island home? Will voters turn out despite the outbreak of illness plaguing their tranquil town? And the even bigger question: Has darkness come to stay on Lantern Beach?

Plan of Action

A missing Navy SEAL. Danger at the boiling point. The ultimate showdown. When Police Chief Cassidy Chambers' husband, Ty, disappears, her world is turned upside down. His truck is discovered with blood inside, crashed in a ditch on Lantern Beach, but he's nowhere to be found. As they launch a manhunt to find him, Cassidy discovers that someone on the island has a deadly obsession with Ty. Meanwhile, Gilead's Cove seems to be imploding. As danger heightens, federal law enforcement officials are called in. The cult's growing threat could lead to the pinnacle standoff of good versus evil. A clear plan of action is needed or the results will be devastating. Will Cassidy find Ty in time, or will she face a gut-wrenching loss? Will Anthony Gilead finally be unmasked for who he really is and be brought to justice? Hundreds of innocent lives are at stake . . . and not everyone will come out alive.

On her way to completing a degree in forensic science, Gabby St. Claire drops out of school and starts her own crime-scene cleaning business. When a routine cleaning job uncovers a murder weapon the police overlooked, she realizes that the wrong person is in jail. She also realizes that crime scene cleaning might be the perfect career for utilizing her investigative skills.

#1 Hazardous Duty
#2 Suspicious Minds
#2.5 It Came Upon a Midnight Crime (novella)
#3 Organized Grime
#4 Dirty Deeds
#5 The Scum of All Fears

HOLLY ANNA PALADIN MYSTERIES:

When Holly Anna Paladin is given a year to live, she embraces her final days doing what she loves most—random acts of kindness. But when one of her extreme good deeds goes horribly wrong, implicating Holly in a string of murders, Holly is suddenly in a different kind of fight for her life. She knows one thing for sure: she only has a short amount of time to make a difference. And if helping the people she cares about puts her in danger, it's a risk worth taking.

THE WORST DETECTIVE EVER:

I'm not really a private detective. I just play one on TV.

Joey Darling, better known to the world as Raven Remington, detective extraordinaire, is trying to separate herself from her invincible alter ego. She played the spunky character for five years on the hit TV show *Relentless*, which catapulted her to fame and into the role of Hollywood's sweetheart. When her marriage falls apart, her finances dwindle to nothing, and her father disappears, Joey finds herself on the Outer Banks of North Carolina, trying to piece together her life away from the limelight. But as people continually mistake her for the character she played on TV, she's tasked with solving real life crimes . . . even though she's terrible at it.

FOG LAKE SUSPENSE

Edge of Peril

When evil descends like fog on a mountain community, no one feels safe. After hearing about a string of murders in a Smoky Mountain town, journalist Harper Jennings realizes a startling truth. She knows who may be responsible—the same person who tried to kill her three years ago. Now Harper must convince the cops to believe her before the killer strikes again. Sheriff Luke Wilder returned to his hometown, determined to keep the promise he made to his dying father. The sleepy tourist area with a tragic past hadn't seen a murder in decades—until now. Keeping the community safe seems impossible as darkness edges closer, threatening to consume everything in its path. As The Watcher grows desperate, Harper and Luke must work together in order to defeat him. But the peril around them escalates, making it clear the killer will stop at nothing to get what he wants.

Margin of Error

Some secrets have deadly consequences. Brynlee Parker thought her biggest challenge would be hiking to Dead Man's Bluff and fulfilling her dad's last wishes. She never thought she'd witness two men being viciously murdered while on a mountainous trail. Even worse, the deadly predator is now hunting her. Boone Wilder wants nothing to do with Dead Man's Bluff, not after his wife died there. But he can't seem to mind his own business when a mysterious out-of-towner burst into his camp store in a frenzied panic. Something—or someone— deadly is out there. The killer's hunger for blood seems to be growing at a brutal pace. Can Brynlee and Boone figure out who's behind these murders? Or will the hurts and secrets from their past not allow for even a margin of error?

Brink of Danger

Ansley Wilder has always lived life on the wild side, using thrills to numb the pain from her past and escape her mistakes. But a near-death experience two years ago changed everything. When another incident nearly claims her life, she turns her thrill-seeking ways into a fight for survival. Ryan Philips left Fog Lake to chase adventure far from home. Now he's returned as the new fire chief in town, but the slower paced life he seeks is nowhere to be found. Not only is a wildfire blazing out of control, but a malicious killer known as "The Woodsman" is enacting crimes that appear accidental. Plus, there seems to be a strange connection with these incidents and his best friend's little sister, Ansley Wilder. As a killer watches their every move and the forest fire threatens to destroy their scenic town, both Ryan and Ansley hover on the brink of danger. One wrong move could send them tumbling over the edge ... permanently.

ABOUT THE AUTHOR

USA Today has called Christy Barritt's books "scary, funny, passionate, and quirky."

Christy writes both mystery and romantic suspense novels that are clean with underlying messages of faith. Her books have won the Daphne du Maurier Award for Excellence in Suspense and Mystery, have been twice nominated for the Romantic Times Reviewers' Choice Award, and have finaled for both a Carol Award and Foreword Magazine's Book of the Year.

She is married to her Prince Charming, a man who thinks she's hilarious—but only when she's not trying to be. Christy is a self-proclaimed klutz, an avid music lover who's known for spontaneously bursting into song, and a road trip aficionado.

When she's not working or spending time with her family, she enjoys singing, playing the guitar, and exploring small, unsuspecting towns where people have no idea how accident-prone she is.

Find Christy online at:
  www.christybarritt.com
  www.facebook.com/christybarritt
  www.twitter.com/cbarritt

Sign up for Christy's newsletter to get information on all of her latest releases here: **www.christybarritt.com/newsletter-sign-up/**

If you enjoyed this book, please consider leaving a review.